INTO THE DARKNESS
Darkness, #1

by K.F. Breene

Website: http://kfbreene.com/
Blog: www.kfbreene.org
Facebook: www.facebook.com/authorKF
Twitter: @KFBreene

Other Titles by K.F. Breene

Skyline Series (Contemporary Romance)
Building Trouble, Book 1
Uneven Foundation, Book 2
Solid Ground, Book 3

Jessica Brodie Diaries (Contemporary Romance)
Back in the Saddle, Book 1 – FREE
Hanging On, Book 2
A Wild Ride, Book 3

Growing Pains (Contemporary Romance)
Lost and Found, Book 1 - FREE
Overcoming Fear, Book 2
Butterflies in Honey, Book 3

Darkness Series (Paranormal Romance)
Into the Darkness, Novella 1
Braving the Elements, Novella 2
On a Razor's Edge, Novella 3
Demons, Novella 4

Contents

Prologue

The little girl fell out of the car door, twisted metal encircling her like protective arms. Dazed, blood dripping down her cheek, she staggered from the wreckage. Too confused to cry, glass crunching under shoeless feet, she paused, staring away from the carnage out at the darkness.

The night held its breath, silence echoing in the wake of massacre.

A spark flared from one of the ruined engines. Heat met the petroleum coated ground. Flame licked the liquid, coaxed to life.

The first wail of a siren wrenched the scene. The hungry flame caught. As the girl stared dumbly, making out shapes in the shadows, fire consumed the twisted bodies of car and human alike. Blue flame skipped along the gravel, a silent predator. Finding a petroleum-covered sock, it climbed up a small leg, reaching for a blood-crusted tutu.

Still the girl stared at the figures moving in the darkness. Human shaped creatures with eyes that caught and threw the light. Large, hulking frames. Silky, dangerous movements.

Heat seared her numb leg, her sensitivity cut off in shock.

"What are you doing?" one of the shapes seethed from deep within the inky shadows. He clutched at an arm, stopping forward movement.

"She'll die."

"She's human. That's what they do. *Leave it.*"

"She is but a child."

"It isn't our concern."

The arm ripped free. "I will not allow a child to burn to death. Not after surviving the impossible. She was fated to live."

"Then why must you save her?"

"Often Fate is struck down by dumb luck."

A shadow charged forth, a black pool among flashing blue and red. The girl did not flinch, unafraid of the large figure rushing her. Still unable to comprehend her danger. Or the death around her.

The tiny body was ripped away from the carnage, flame smothered in black leather.

Chapter One

"Sasha? What is it?"

My face slipped off my palm and jerked my shoulders toward the table. Blinking away the daydream, I tore my eyes away from the balmy day peeking out of the window. My boyfriend, Jared, stared at me out of a cute, boyish face, his eyebrows quirked quizzically.

"Not a thing," I answered with an easy smile. "Where we headed tonight?"

He crinkled his nose. "You've been daydreaming all day. Was it that imaginary guy from yesterday? The invisible male model strolling down the street?" He laughed at the absurdity of what he'd said.

I threw a wadded up napkin at him with a smile. "Be quiet, you. You go spreading that story around and everyone'll think I'm crazy."

"Nah. They already know it." He sipped his coffee, his brown eyes sparkling above the rim of his cup.

"Actually, smart guy, I was thinking about that test." I rolled my eyes. "I hate tests. Why don't they just trust me that I don't know the material and give me a passing grade anyway? It would be so much easier on everyone."

Jared laughed and leaned back in his chair. "You want help?"

"Argh!"

"What are you, a pirate?"

I smirked and sipped my coffee. "I guess. I'm certainly not going to pass it without you."

He shook his head and laughed. "You need to have some faith in yourself."

"That's your job. I stick to reality."

He shook his head and got up to pay the check. My thoughts immediately went right back to the enigma. That man.

He'd been gliding down the street, movements lithe and graceful, unshakable confidence in every step. His powerfully muscular body belied an age ten years older than his youthful looking mid-twenties. My eyes stuck to him like a butterfly's wings in honey. Something about him drew me. Pulled my attention and then tugged at my body.

It wasn't just that he was breathtakingly handsome with perfect features. Which he was. But there was something else, too. A deadly grace—like a dancer—etched his every movement. His muscles moved in perfect harmony, a chorus of power and might. Dominating. Oh-so-god-damned-sexy.

As he neared, he drew me like a magnet. I could feel my body responding, wanting to go to him. Wanting to take those three short steps and touch his body. Smile up at him. Anything to get his attention; to get his praise.

Eyes the color of sparkling onyx had swung my way, feeling the weight of my stare and answering. I devoured the challenge in his eyes. Answered it with a yearning that consumed my entire being in a way I'd never felt before. A way I'd never even heard someone could feel. Like a deep ache burning in the pit of my stomach and spilling over every inch of my frame, I tingled with the need for him. I pounded with it, the beat of my heart throbbing in a few choice parts of my body.

It had taken Jared's confused tug to jerk me away—yank my head out of the strange fantasy I'd conjured up. When I'd turned back, he was gone.

Jared had asked what I'd smiled dreamily at.

I hadn't remembered doing that, obviously. And I *definitely* didn't remember giving empty air a greeting. But apparently, if Jared was to be believed (and being that he was smart, talented, and always on top of things, he probably should), I had been following the travels of the wind as it passed us by. Wind being visible? That was strange. Even stranger? Muttering largely incoherent words at it.

Yes Jared, that *is* odd. I don't know what came over me. Ha-ha…

It wasn't funny.

What it *was,* however, was an example of the kinds of things I had religiously tried to keep from people. This was a secret box item, and I had long since learned my lesson on that subject. A "humor me" psych evaluation at the request of my foster parents put a pretty fine point on it. I'd only been ten years old at the time. I'd had to get street savvy really quickly after that—they'd never adopted me, they could give me back. And *would* give me back if I showed signs of mental instability.

This recent episode meant I had to put a little more distance between Jared and I, which sucked because I'd already managed to wedge a hefty amount of space between us as it was. I wanted to get closer and fully trust him, sharing a deeper level of intimacy; but shortly after we'd first gotten intimate, I'd explained about the strange things I saw in the shadows. I'd told him an item or two that I kept in my secret box. He'd responded by worriedly asking if I had a counselor. When he learned I didn't, he tried to set one up. He only meant well, but if I didn't want to end up in a place with twenty-four hour surveillance, I had to zip the lip. Even with him.

"Sasha?"

"Ta da!" I threw some jazz hands Jared's way.

"God, you're weird." He grabbed my jacket and waited for me to gulp down the rest of my coffee.

"I know you are, but what am I?" I smiled up at Jared's shaking head, angling my face up for a kiss. "Good one, right? When's the last time you heard that one?"

"Don't know. When's the last time you said it?" He gave me a quick peck and directed me toward the door.

"Touché, my good man. Touché."

Two hours later my eyes were crossed and my head hurt. Why the hell was calculus important, anyway? How was I possibly going to need this in my everyday life? I should've taken statistics for the math credits. Although, same question applied, and that teacher was a huge jerk, so…

"Give up?" Jared leaned back with a sigh, easy breezy. What the heck a smart guy was doing with a dummy like me was anyone's guess.

Zip the lip.

"Where was I when the man behind the curtain was giving out brains?" I closed my book and tossed it on the floor. The dull thunk was strangely gratifying.

"You hadn't left the wildness clinic yet. Let's remember who talked me into skydiving."

"Not my fault that you don't know how to live." I threw my pencil at my backpack. "I don't think I can absorb anymore. My brain hurts."

"We could always...take your mind off of things..." Jared rubbed my back, his shy and subtle way of hinting that he wanted to have a little nookie. It was so cute.

Giggling, because I was always down for a little naked fun, I stretched for his zipper. Embarrassed but excited, Jared put his hands to his sides on the bed and braced himself, wanting me to take the lead. His breath hitched as I tugged at his zipper. His eyes hooded.

Reaching in with a wicked grin I captured my prize. I met his lips as I slid my palm against him, steel encased in luxury velvet. His kiss tasted like coffee and spearmint, his tongue shy and reserved.

I backed off seductively—I tried for seduction, anyway—and slowly bent. He sucked in a huge breath as I took him in my mouth. I loved his uncontrolled moan as the sensations overwhelmed him. It was in this moment that I felt sexy and masterful, taking him beyond his reasonable mind to a place that was raw and wild. I wished we could stay here, two first-timers pushing our boundaries together.

Except he was a younger guy and couldn't really hold back, and I was a younger girl and needed a little finesse. Troubled times.

Speaking of time, I didn't have much of it. I worked at my shirt while keeping up the suction. I'd just gotten the last button undone, ready to rip the thing off and get in position quickly, when—

"Ohhhhhhhh *God!*"

I gagged. I couldn't help it.

"Hmmm, sorry baby." Jared smiled in relaxation as he sighed in relief, then tucked himself away and fell back against his pillows. "You're just so good at that. Are you sure you aren't practicing sex in class or something?"

"Sex classes a la Jared, yeah." I cleaned myself up as his lids got heavy. My body, hot and tingling, begged me to continue our forays. "Is that… Are we…um…done?"

He laughed with a deep sigh. "I think I'm just going to take a quick nap, if that's okay?"

"Oh. Yeah, totally. Definitely." I bobbed my head, feeling a little awkward with my shirt hanging open. I stared down at him as I buttoned up, feeling a tiny smile bud at his absolute contentment.

I was lucky to have him. Peaceful and easygoing, he always took my slips in sanity with a *laissez-faire* attitude. I wished I could fully open up to him like I wanted to. He was my *first,* damn it— having met him my sophomore year in high school, he was my first kiss, first real relationship, first sexual partner, and first meaningful friend. And he was kind of *my everything* these days.

A familiar pallor washed over me as I thought about keeping the closest person in my life at an arm's reach. That I had to continue on in a weird half-life, in which I kept all the important things hidden behind a veil of secrecy. Saying I was alone was like calling the surface of the sun warm. Saying I was lonely…well, I couldn't seem to find a way to fill the void my childhood had created. I'd lost my parents and brother young, the sole survivor in a freak, five car pileup. Everyone had died. Every single person. Killed on impact, or shortly thereafter in a bright blaze seen for miles. I'd been found in a nearby park with a bad gash to the head, small burns on my legs, and severely in shock. To this day, no one has been able to explain it.

I didn't remember a thing.

Having no aunts or uncles, no other family, I ended up in foster care knowing I would spend my life fending for myself. I'd gotten lucky, both to escape the crash, and to end up with two well-rounded people and their two averagely bratty children. I fit in with them as any fifth wheel might, and they tried really hard to make me feel at home; but...well, I was the only foster kid in our upper-middle class suburbia, and though I did have some friends growing up, they never let me forget that I didn't have deep roots. Their parents couldn't give them away if we got caught shoplifting. Mine could. And might've.

I was forever an army of one, having no one in my life to give me the unconditional love other kids took for granted. My accomplishments were praised with a placating smile and a nod or two where my foster brother or sister would get jubilant commendation and shrieks of delight. I had one picture on the fridge that never changed, pushed off to the side and half covered by multilayers of pictures brought home from the children that belonged. And only a fool would be upset by any of that, because I'd been in a good home with a good family, and sent to good schools, where others were in an orphanage on the bad side of town. I thanked my luck every day. I'd endure a helluva lot more for the chance in life I got.

If only the parent issue was my biggest problem.

Why was I seeing imaginary people? To this day, I didn't know if any of that was real. I mean, how could they be? Eyes that reflected the light like a nocturnal animal? Invisible people no one else saw?

I was cracked and too afraid to confide in anyone, especially Jared. He was really all I had—my foster parents moved away when all the kids went to college. If he knew I was constantly hallucinating then…well, I didn't want another appointment for a psych evaluation, I'd say that much.

I lightly traced a finger down Jared's cheek, then bent over and gave him a light kiss. "Okay, well, pick me up later?"

"Yeah," he mumbled, drifting off to sleep.

Oh man, I loved this time of night! I exited my one-bedroom apartment as the sun shook hands with the horizon. The cool breeze tickled my face, making me sigh in contentment, picking up the soft smell of roses dotting the front lawn of the apartment complex.

Jared waited in his convertible by the curb wearing the spiffy button-up shirt I loved. "Hey, babe," I said, slipping into the front seat. I leaned over for a kiss then buckled myself in. "Where to?"

"I have a great evening planned."

"Oh?"

The corner of his lips tweaked, trying to suppress a smug grin. He shrugged. "Have to give you a reason to…come home with me, don't I? Make up for…things."

I couldn't help laughing. His smirk turned into a full, gleaming smile. With a blast of power, the car lurched forward, pushing me back into the seat. I put my hands up in glee, the wind almost visible as it pushed against my palms and wound its way through my fingers. A girl nearly dying in a car crash should be deathly afraid of cars. Should be…

My teeth became a bug screen and my laughter bubbled up like a bottle of champagne. But I wasn't afraid. Not of much. In high school, I'd take a dare with a smile. I was always the fearless one, ready for any challenge. Maybe I should've thought a few things through, but…well, life was in the journey. The wilder, the better.

An exhilarating ride later, Jared said, "Here we are," as he turned into a gravel road leading up to a parking lot nestled in the woods. A seemingly plain and simple house waited off to the side, the wraparound porch glowing from the many lit windows.

"My-oh-my, pulling out all the stops, are we? What's the occasion?" I threaded my fingers through his after I climbed from the car.

"Have to take care of my girl."

I let my body lean against his as we made our way to the restaurant's porch, the dark woods around us deep and quiet. Like they always did, my eyes swept to the side, searching.

"What's up?" Jared asked, following my gaze.

Adrenaline pierced my chest. *Stop looking for imaginary people!*

"Oh, nothing! Spooky, though, huh?"

Jared squeezed my shoulders. "Nah, biggest thing up here is a raccoon. I'll protect you!"

"I don't know, I hear those raccoons are feisty."

Laughing, we entered the restaurant.

I walked out an hour and a half later with a firm hold on my stuffed tummy. "Why do I always hate myself after a good meal?" I mumbled.

"I feel pregnant." Jared slipped on a light jacket against the chill of the evening. "Let's just hope it doesn't turn gassy."

"Eww, Jared! You're so gross!"

"Good thing I have a convertible or I'd fart you out of the car."

"Would you stop?" I slapped his arm playfully. "Where to?"

"We're not going to a carnival, I'll tell you that much. Dancing is out, too. God, I'm *stuffed!*"

As we stepped off the porch, happily swaying into each other, something tickled my awareness. Almost as if someone called my name, I glanced off to the right, my gaze trying to pierce the syrupy shadows between the trees. A small tug in the center of my chest jerked my body sideways.

Shadows moved, shifted. A huge expanse of shoulder swiveled. A leg stepped to the right. A body tucked further into the darkness, the shadows wrapping it in a nearly invisible cloak.

It was like walking into the kitchen after you'd just left it, having had to close a randomly opened cabinet door, and then seeing every cabinet suddenly standing wide open. A shot of pure adrenaline punched me.

Someone was there!

"Oh my God…"

An overwhelming desire to join that person washed through me. I couldn't think through the intense need to go to him. Like an alcoholic after a binge, my heart hammered and my hands shook; the desire to walk that direction so strong, I couldn't focus.

"What's up?" Jared asked, stopping with me. "Do you see something?"

The man was looking back, I knew he was. Just as I knew it was a man. And he was *right there.* The answer to my questions was so close. Waiting there, not moving. Staring. I had to get to him. I had to touch him, see if he was real. *Had to.*

"Let's go for a walk," I murmured, my feet jerking to a start.

"What? Sasha, are you okay? What's…?" Jared's words ended in a hiss.

My skin prickled, a surge of fear blasting, and then sliding right off me.

"Just a peek…" I heard myself say. The pull gripped me, had sweat drenching my hairline. "Have to…"

"Sasha, *no!*"

My body whipped around so fast tree branches and stars blurred in my vision. Jared had my arm and started dragging me toward the car.

Clothes rustled by that tree, a boot scraped against the dirt, the unseen person shifting, seething at Jared's manhandling me. Wanting me out of harm's way.

How could I possibly know that?

"C'mon, Sasha. This is…we need to go." Jared hurriedly shuffled me toward the car. "*Quick.*"

"But…" I was shoved into the seat, the door slamming a second later as Jared jogged to his side of the car. The key jammed into the ignition and we were off, tires splashing gravel at the line of parked cars. "Careful!"

White knuckles gripping the steering wheel, Jared took the turn into the street way too fast, nearly running the car off the road into a steep ravine. "Jared, look out!"

He swerved, our vision going white in the face of an oncoming car. His car squealed as he jerked the wheel. Tires on the right side dropped off the lip of the road. I clutched at the dashboard, trying to pull a Superman and direct the car with superhuman strength. Jared jerked the wheel again, his chest heaving, hard lines around his eyes. We took another turn too fast.

"Jared! What's going on? Why are you so freaked out?"

As if waking from paralysis, Jared glanced over, eyes quickly going back to the road. He rolled his shoulders. His knuckles slowly returned to normal color. "I don't know. Wow. That was weird. All of a sudden it felt like we were going to die or something. Like, get killed kind of die, not like…you know."

I didn't, but I didn't say anything, because I'd had the opposite reaction. *Secret box.*

The farther we got from the restaurant, driving faster than we should've, the more relaxed Jared became. The hard lines around his eyes softened, and his smile peeked through. He reached for my hand as he took a curve, reentering the noise and clutter of civilization.

"Almost there."

I couldn't help but think his crazy reaction was to what was in the woods. Did he feel it? Did he feel that tug, too, but instead of exciting him, it scared him?

Did I have proof the shadows were real?

My mind raced as we sped along a deserted road on the outskirts of town. The cracked sidewalks and dingy overhangs were devoid of the usual homeless. Which was weird, but not altogether noteworthy. The current predicament, however…

Should I ask him if he saw anything? Or felt something? Would I sound crazy?

But what if he'd been noticing my weird reactions to empty air lately and was scared for me? What if he was trying to save me from myself?

Did that thought, in itself, sound crazy? Oh God…*am I crazy??*

I sucked in a nervous breath to ask when the tire jounced over something in the street and exploded like a cannon. We swerved wildly, Jared ripping his hand from me as the car careened left.

I watched in horror as a tree enlarged within the confines of the windshield. A breathless split-second and my body slammed forward with a shriek of twisting metal. The car flew sideways, slamming against the curb, rocking back and forth like a lullaby.

There was one moment of absolute quiet except for the hissing steam spewing from the radiator.

"Holy crap," I said, out of breath. "That came outta nowhere, huh? Tree one, monkey nothing." I struggled with the airbag.

Jared stared, wide-eyed, out of the splintered windshield.

"Hey," I whispered softly, touching his shoulder, "are you okay?"

Like a man who had been body snatched, his head swung in my direction. His jaw hung slack and his eyes were glazed over. God had written, "Nobody's home" all over his forehead.

"Hey, baby." I shook him gently. "You okay?"

He blinked. "I just crashed my car."

A bark of laughter escaped my mouth before I could rearrange my face back into a mask of concern. "Yes, sweetie. But you have insurance. It's okay. As long as you're okay?"

Like a door on a rusty hinge, his head swung back toward the cracked windshield, looking out at a jumble of hood wrestling a tree.

The tree was winning.

Alright, then.

I took a big breath and glanced around us. We weren't in a good neighborhood and cell phone service was spotty at best. Waiting for a tow-truck here was dicey, especially in a convertible where we couldn't lock ourselves in. Well, we *could,* but I had the sneaking suspicion villains could penetrate invisible roofs.

Walking out of here was equally bad, however. This was the worst part of town for missing persons and violence. People that walked through the streets here sometimes turned up the next day, or even a week later, claiming to have lost their memory. Usually they were weak, suffering blood loss, and sometimes suffered from strange maladies that cleared up without the use of medicine.

Most honest, hard-working citizens cursed drugs for this, of course. And even though it often happened that normal people—men and women both—reported these strange occurrences, it was a college town. Not much more needed to be said.

Regardless, if there was something fishy going on in these parts, I didn't want to know about it. I had enough fodder for my secret box. I didn't need more crazy to wedge between me and everyone else.

But the question remained: Walk or hang out? Stay here and let crazy find us, or hump out of here like an army man, able to run if we needed to. Able to fight. Able to…I dunno…scream or something.

I climbed out of the car, wiping my chin of drool. *Thank you airbag, for the sucker punch.*

"Sasha, where are you going?" Jared sank further into his seat like a ground hog in a hole. He was nose diving into shock.

"C'mon, baby," I said, helping him out of the car. "Let's find a well-lit café and call a tow-truck."

Jared looked at his smashed car, shaking his head in loss. "But my car is here…"

"I know, baby. We'll just go get help, and then come back for it, okay? No one will try to steal it, I promise."

He stared at me like he didn't believe me. "Okay," he whined.

Chapter Two

We took off at a fast walk, Jared limping by my side.

"Where is everybody?" I asked myself, scanning the streets ahead of us. Then risking a glance behind.

The street lights in this area worked as often as they didn't, leaving the deserted street in a murky kind of gloom. The stale hum of distant cars seemed out of place in this weird vacuum. It was like this couple of blocks was stagnant; the night holding its breath.

"Invisible men and strangely vacant city blocks," I muttered to myself. "Oh yeah, this is normal, all right.

I stopped at the corner of Farrel and Market, eyeing my options. Straight on was a dark sidewalk with only two working lights. Alleyways dumped out into the street, giving dangerous street urchins multiple places to hide. If we went right, it would be safer, with limited outlets and hiding spots, but also less traffic to come to our aid if something awaited halfway down. And in this neck of the woods, something almost assuredly awaited half-way down. Jared couldn't run, and I was barely able to support him as it was.

I opted for the hope that the larger thoroughfare would bring a car, or dare I hope, a cab, that might help us. Or at least keep people from openly mugging us.

"Okay, baby, we're almost there." I started forward, muttering, "Kind of."

Fifteen minutes into our walk, we were halfway along the still-empty street. Garbage littered the sidewalk, and old crates, half rotted, dotted the alleyways. Shopping carts stood idly by, blankets, cans, and other manner of survival items left unattended.

"But where are the inhabitants?" I mused aloud.

"Scattered or dead."

I jumped and clutched Jared. It was a voice out of a nightmare, rough and low. We stood in the mouth of an alleyway under a blackened street light. Darkness gaped in front of me. I could feel more than see a presence.

"Wandered a little far from home, hey pet?" By the laughter in that voice, it was clear we were the red ball to his dodge ball game.

Darkness moved. Coalesced. A shape stepped out of the black, huge and lumbering, circling around us. Oh crap.

Another shape stepped forward after him, just as big, heavy arms poised to his sides. This one passed to the left.

They were monstrous. Both. Easily over six-and-a-half feet tall, pushing seven.

Freaking crap!

"What shall we do with you, little pet?" the first man asked, crossing behind us.

"*Oh,* yes. That's nice." Jared's hands dropped away from me like fluffy clouds. His expression turned dreamy. The guy looked like he was at a sauna rather than about to get mugged by two ginormous men!

"Jared!" I whispered furiously. "Keep with me, baby."

"She hasn't tried to run from us, Charles. What do you think about that?" the dangerous man droned as he stepped closer, herding me toward the alley.

"That means she's feisty, right?" Charles asked, emulating the other guy and lazily stepping closer.

My skin broke out in goose bumps with his proximity, weird tingles creeping up my arms and legs. The sensations, largely pleasurable, hazed my brain, creeping into private places and producing an extremely terrible feeling of desire given the situation. I blinked in confusion, trying desperately to clear my head.

"I get this one," Charles said, taking a step closer. "Called it."

"Figures," the other mumbled, his attention slipping past me to a patient and gooey-eyed Jared. "Mine has already succumbed. Look at him. He's begging for it. Weak-willed, boring human."

"You must lay it on too thick, that's why."

"What do you plan to do?" I asked in a firm voice, a surge of adrenaline boosting my courage. They'd started acting like we wouldn't fight them off. Which was just silly. Sure, they were colossal and I, solely, represented our combat unit, but I did not intend to be mugged without at least putting up some resistance. Despite the weird urges of my Stockholm Syndrome-corrupted body, I did not intend for this to be easy for them.

"Screw you. Bite you. Maybe bleed you, depending on the time," Charles said patiently. The other guy moved back around, aiming for Jared.

"A whole day planned then, lovely," I muttered without meaning to.

I clutched Jared tighter, unsure why the hell he was groping me, and took a step back, trying to get Charles to step with us. My half-cocked plan was to make a hole between them large enough that I could shoot us out into the middle of the street. If I had any luck we'd get hit by a car—at least then it would be forced to stop and help.

"Smells like you like that idea," Charles grinned.

I swatted Jared's hands away from my butt. We took one more step back, each large shadow stepping with us, stalking us like predators. One of Jared's hands reached between my legs, making me jump. Before I could turn that movement into a dart between the domineering shapes, the Danger Shadow reached out, faster than expected, and swept Jared from my side.

"No!" I screamed, reaching for him.

Large hands swung me toward the alley. My back bumped the wall as Charles pushed in close. Six-five or more, his arms braced around me. His torso was robust and barrel-shaped, no fat to speak of.

He bent down to my neck and inhaled deeply. "You smell like fresh rain in the forest. No, wait. Warm, chocolate cake. Yum. I've never had a human that smelled as good as you. You don't have to be coaxed. *Delicious.*"

"Gross. Get away from me!" I pushed at his giant chest, panic thankfully starting to fight my faux arousal.

"You're squirrely. Seriously, you'll like this, human. I know what I'm doing. Girls rave." His hand landed on my shoulder with implied intimacy.

A wild urge rose up from deep inside, the part of me that always found fast cars and high-impact sports exhilarating, unfurling gratefully from my usually carefully controlled persona. It screamed one word like a siren.

Fight!

I punched Charles in the chest as hard as I could, jarring him away from my neck. His face backed up, eyebrows dipping low. "Well that wasn't very nice. Or do you like rough play, because usually humans aren't this feisty......"

"Yes, exactly, roughly screwing bullies on street corners is my gig," I said through clenched teeth. I kicked his shin. A stab of pain screamed up my leg.

He grabbed my hair and yanked my head back with an assessing glance, startling a cry.

Cue hysterics.

I slapped at his face like a five-year-old, panicking. Then turned palms into fists and tried again. My fists splashed against a hard, square jaw. Crying out, gritting my teeth against the pain, I tried to poke an eye, aiming for vulnerable spots. He didn't seem to have any.

What was this guy made of, rocks?

I was losing the fight. Fear started to drip down my body like acid. I welcomed it, chasing away the weird, completely unnatural arousal that would not go *away*. But he wasn't relenting and I was no match for his size. Hell, not many people, women nor men, were a match for this giant.

Tears near the surface, brain scrabbling for some way out of this, I heard, "Stop."

Like a whip-crack, the command echoed through the alley. Charles froze. A dissatisfied whine came from somewhere across the way, but I couldn't focus on that. I couldn't even focus on Charles, still too close. My attention was sucked toward the speaker.

"Release her."

My head dropped forward as Charles let go of my hair and stepped back quickly, dropping his hands to his sides like a kid trying not to be caught ransacking the cookies. A massive shape dominated the mouth of the alley. The glow from distant streetlights partially illuminated a breathtaking face. His body, poised, ready to fight, stood tall and firm, strength and power tempered with deadly grace.

It was him! The guy walking under the street light yesterday!

Something inside me sparked and started to glow, the draw of him once again tugging at me. His eyes swept past me to the other side of the alleyway. I followed their journey.

And then squeaked in horrified shock.

Danger Shadow stood with a ramrod straight back. He'd frozen like Charles. My boyfriend, who never even wanted to have sex with the light on if he could help it, and preferred the missionary position, was railing against the stranger with a serene expression.

What. The. *Hell?* Charles' words suddenly made a lot more sense. My not responding like normal humans made no sense at all.

"You're supposed to be securing the area," the newcomer continued through my confused haze, his voice tight with anger. "We've had territory breaches every day this past week. They're trying to take down as many of our people as possible. I'm sure I don't have to remind you that they have a powerful mage. So I ask you again, what are you doing here, playing around with a couple of humans?"

"We scouted and came up empty, Boss. Whatever it was is long gone," Charles said with strain, hand cupping the bulge in his jeans. "Then we kinda…got distracted."

"You should've reported that information, rather than sought out pleasure," the newcomer growled. He unconsciously flexed, his pecs becoming mountains. He sported useable, workable muscle.

"My fault, Boss," the guy with Jared said. "I needed something to take the edge off. Charles was starting to get on my nerves."

"Kind of a dick thing to say, bro," Charles muttered.

My mouth dropped open. What the hell was going on? Did someone slip me acid, or something? Was the circus in town and no one mentioned it?

Ebony eyes flashed to me. "Why is she lucid?" The Boss's eyes flayed Charles. "Pain is forbidden, unless requested. Judging by her shrieks, it was not requested."

"I'm at full strength!" Charles bleated. "I have been for a while! I've never met a human that didn't go for it. I thought she was just roll-playing or something. How am I supposed to know…?"

Charles sputtered to a stop within the hard glare of the boss. He lowered his head. "Sorry, Boss."

"I'm at full, too," the other guy noted. "You can see what it's doing to this guy."

"I want to speak with the girl," the Boss said, stepping forward. Charles hastened away to the side, giving him room.

"I hope this is an incredibly screwed up nightmare," I managed.

The newcomer—the Boss—stopped in front of me. His eyes glued to my face. "Why are you not frightened of me?"

Great question. I had no idea. I just knew that I absolutely wasn't. Not even a little bit. I faced off against his size, pure brawn and bulk with a killer's grace, and wanted to melt against his thick, muscled chest. It was as strange and not normal as Jared's sudden interest in men.

So I lied. "Because you're not scary."

His calculating black eyes analyzed me. "You are human."

"Ten points to you for your powers of observation. Bloody good show, Watson," I retorted automatically.

"How do you know me?"

"I don't. Look, let us go so I can go home and try to find some amnesia pills. I have no idea what's going on, what you've done to him, and why I'm not normal, but if this weird shit goes on any longer I am going to self-destruct. I can feel it."

"You saw me last night. You saw me earlier this evening. You show up here, in my territory. You engage with my crew. You have some sort of strange effect on my senses. I don't believe in coincidence. Who are you working for? Tell me, and I may let you live."

A shiver started at my head and worked down my body, flash freezing my blood. It stupidly never occurred to me that death was a variable with this man. Although, nothing made much sense, anymore. My brain had hit the snooze button and disengaged.

Then something struck me. "What do you mean earlier this evening?" My mind recalled the shape near the tree; the motionless stranger, watching me as I watched him. "That was you…"

"You can see my dilemma."

I shook my head slowly. Then started babbling. "I didn't know that was you! I couldn't make out features. Or a shape, even. We aren't in your territory on purpose! I don't even *like* your territory. It's the ghetto. We ran over something. The car hit a tree. Honest! We are trying to get somewhere safe to call for a tow truck. We were just passing through and those guys stopped us. I go to community college—I don't even have a real job!"

"I sense honesty. Odd." His expression turned thoughtful. "I'll watch you. If you come looking again, I'll kill you."

I answered by gulping. Loudly.

The Boss turned to the others. "Wipe their memories. Do a thorough job. Deposit them and deal with the car, if indeed there has been a crash."

"Can I have a crack at the girl before we take them back?" Charles asked hopefully, still holding his bulge through his pants. He looked pained. "I'm pretty sure I can bring her around..."

I got an assessing glance. Some decision tugged down the corners of the Boss' mouth, his expression mildly confused. Finally, he said, "No. Leave her. I want to see you back within the hour."

Chapter Three

I awoke with a groggy head sometime in the mid-morning. I lay on top of the covers in Jared's bed, completely clothed. I even had my shoes on. Jared lay next to me, face down, partially clothed.

I labored to sit up, putting a hand to my fuzzy head. I felt like I'd been drinking.

I thought back to the night before. I remembered dinner. We'd each had a glass of wine. We'd walked outside. Something had spooked Jared—

A memory nudged my brain. I clutched at it, scrabbling on the slippery thing, trying to fit it into place. All I caught was wisps.

Sighing, struggling to remember what day it was, I checked my watch, remembered I didn't have one on, and looked around for my phone. It was across the room, sticking haphazardly out of my purse. On the ground.

I never put my purse on the ground. I always put it on a chair or counter top to keep the bottom clean. I'm anal like that.

Another memory wobbled just out of reach, feathering my awareness. There were pieces missing from last night—like everything after dinner!

"Sasha?" Jared roused, lifting onto his forearms and looking around the room. His head turned to me, eyes bleary.

"Good morning. I think," I said as I completed my zigzag to my handbag.

"What time is it?"

"I don't know. I was just getting up to check. You need to get a clock."

"What happened last night? Did we drink? How'd we get home?"

I snatched my phone and touched it. "Nine-oh-five. Huh. Seems later."

"I wanna fuck."

I froze, my phone still in front of my face. Jared did not talk like that, all husky and labored. He had never referred to sex as anything other than love-making.

I heard rustling behind me and turned, slowly, incredulous. He sat in the middle of the bed, his erection in his hand. "Come over here baby, I wanna screw you."

My mouth dropped open. Wide eyed, I walked on wooden legs, a smile not far from my lips wondering if this was a joke.

"No, stop there," he said, hunger burning in his eyes.

I halted, as instructed, with baited breath, allowing his eyes to rake over my body. My arousal spiked, this new spice kind of exciting. Like role playing. Dirty talk had been on my list of "To Try's" but Jared always got embarrassed immediately.

He wasn't embarrassed now.

"Strip. Slowly."

Feeling a thrill of anticipation, I slowly worked my buttons on my blouse, feeling air raise bumps on my skin as the fabric shimmied down my body. I let my bra fall a moment later, exposing my B-cup breasts.

"Yes, that's right. Beautiful," Jared praised.

With a growing smile I slowly worked my skirt down my legs, then my panties.

"That's right," Jared murmured in that stranger's voice, full of need. "Spread your legs. Yeah, that's it. Now touch yourself. Good. How does that feel?"

"Good," I answered in a breathy voice.

"Do it faster. I want to hear it."

I let my head fall back, working my body into a fever pitch.

"Good girl. Now climb up onto the bed."

I wasted no time, giddy. I lay on my back in front of him. His eyes scanned my body, illuminated with a manic urgency. Suddenly Jared had turned into a sex starved creature.

That damn fluttering kissed my brain again, nudging me to remember something I was forgetting. Then Jared dove between my legs, blacking out thought all together.

I closed my eyes as my foot hit the pavement, the chill of the night reaching out to greet me. The sun was just tucking behind the horizon. Shadows reached, long arms spreading wide, covering the earth in a welcoming blanket.

Jared stepped out around me. "Do you want to just walk through the park?" He turned the corner of his apartment building toward his car. "Maybe just get some fresh air?"

"Yeah, sure."

"What the…?" Jared's voice cut off.

I hurried in his direction, only to slow with an absurd amount of blinking as I stared at the lime green station wagon parked in his spot. Jared was holding a note in one hand and a business card in the other.

"What did we *do* last night?" he asked with a trembling voice.

Fear tingled my scalp as I stepped up next to him, peering over his shoulder at the shaking note in his hand.

Dear Self,
I wrecked my car last night. It is in David's Body Shop. Here is his card. Insurance was notified. This is a loaner. Be more careful next time.
Signed,
Disappointed Me

Memories fluttered, battering against my brain. There was something there. Something to do with the car. It was just out of reach. I couldn't quite grasp the memory.

"I remember dinner." He shook his head. "I remember walking out. That's it. Walking down the steps holding your hand. Then…nothing." His eyes probed mine searchingly. "You didn't spike my drink to shake things up, did you? Slip me Ecstasy or something?"

I took a step back. All I could manage was, "What?"

"I just… I don't know. I mean, why else wouldn't I remember… And all the sex today…"

Forcing my breath in deep, even puffs, I used a calm tone. "I don't remember anything, either. You think I like waking up with dirt all over my back, as if I was scraped against the ground?

You think that's a good situation for a girl? How the hell would I even navigate you? You weigh fifty pounds more than I do! Think about what the hell you're saying before you start throwing verbal stones, basically saying I'm a shady, untrustworthy creep! Comments like that will get you dumped, quick!"

So, not as calmly as I would've liked, but I made my point.

The breath went out of Jared's lungs. "Yeah." He glanced back at the note. "Well, I'll call this number. See if this is a prank or what." Shaking his head in defeat, he stepped away as he dug out his phone.

"I'll wait at the bench," I muttered, still taken aback by Jared's mistrust. I had no idea he thought of me that way. That he would suspect I'd do something so disgusting in a strange pursuit of this supposed reckless lifestyle. As a person who always followed the rules so as not to be noticed, I found the allegation as absurd as it was offensive.

I meandered to my familiar waiting spot in the park, a stone bench in the middle of a large copse of trees at the edge of his apartment complex. It was lush and secluded, rarely visited by anyone besides those looking for a place their dog could poop. I could partially see the evening sky, a couple stars fighting twilight before full night fell. A soft breeze tickled my nose, pleasing me with a spring floral bouquet.

It was then that I felt the disquiet. Something nudging my senses. It was like a weird tug on my chest. I peered into the shadows between two large trees, following the feeling.

Nothing moved. There wasn't even a flicker. But I could feel it. I could feel the pull of it, whatever it was. I could feel its presence sucking me in.

Another item for the secret box, probably. Imaginary people. I would end up in a padded cell one of these days.

"Sasha."

I jumped so high I nearly fell off the stone seat. "Jesus, Jared! I didn't hear you."

I stood to greet him. "What'd you find out?" I brushed myself off. It was a futile effort. I was still wearing the clothes from the night before, which had dirt smears ground in. "What did we do? Play flag football or something?"

Jared's gaze caught on my cleavage. He extended a hand slowly, reaching under my skirt.

"What are you…?"

"Just real quick," he muttered, his voice back to heavy and husky, the need overriding his logic.

Stunned mute, I stayed still; a strange fantasy of doing this outside competed with embarrassment.

Was that me giggling? What had gotten into me?

"C'mon, baby." Jared wrapped his body around mine, one hand running down my back and cupping my butt, the other working at his zipper.

"Oh my god!" With a wicked smile I peered out through the heavy bushes, seeing no one around. I couldn't stop giggling! I squeezed my eyes shut with a wide smile. *I can't believe I'm doing this!*

"Okay, but...hurry!" I said excitedly.

I giggled again as my lust sparked, clutching onto him. As he readied himself, suddenly a strange feeling came over me. Intense guilt. Like I was harming someone. Adulterous.

With a weight on my chest tugging sideways, impeding breath, my gaze swung left. The shadows moved, dim light flickering off a giant form. Luminescent eyes caught and reflected the light. A face so handsome it hardly looked real was staring at me. *Seething.*

Bat's wings now, flapping at my memories. I knew that man, felt connected with him somehow. I knew that unbelievably handsome, earth shattering face. Those deep, dark, penetrating eyes. It was right there. It was right at the edges of my awareness.

Why did it feel like knowing him was the most important thing in my life?

As Jared kissed my neck, guilt unlike I'd ever felt settled down on me like snowflakes, melting into my skin. The stranger took one step closer. To claim me. To claim what was his.

But that was just crazy. *This was all just fucking crazy!*

My mind warped, unable to handle what was happening. Unable to handle the burning of my body.

I broke away from Jared and ran. Sprinted away. I couldn't handle the confusing surety and absolute conviction that I belonged with a perfect stranger. That I was meant to be with him.

I didn't even know *him!*

My secret box had lit on fire and was burning my life down around me.

Chapter Four

I huddled on my bed later that night with my knees pulled up to my chest. Thinking. Focusing on what it was I couldn't remember. It was there, hovering around my conscious mind. Nudging me. Waiting for me to pay attention. To remember. It was the key to that insane situation in the park.

I flung my wet hair out of my face, pulled the sleeves of my pajamas over my hands, and glanced out the window.

The stranger waited. Outside, he watched, staring up at my shaded windows, just wanting me to know he was there. He was waiting for me to come down to him. He had the same questions I did—I was certain he felt the same things.

How did I know this? I just did. And that scared the crap out of me!

"Get a grip, Sasha!" I exhaled nosily, lightly rocking back and forth. There was no way in hell I was going outside. Not with Jared's strange desires, our inability to remember the night before, a stranger stalking me, and shadows magically coming to life—

I mentally tried to trap the memory. Shadows, arousal, Jared's car—why wouldn't it come clear? It was like a mental block shielding the memories from my awareness. They were there, behind a thick veil, I just had to find a way to them.

I shook my head, shoving aside the presence I felt loitering outside my apartment like a creep and settled into my bed. I doubted sleep would come, but I might as well try. It was midnight and I had to get up early for a test.

My eyes snapped open. I looked around wildly, my room was still and quiet. The red letters on the clock read 4:09. I'd been asleep for four hours.

Drenched in sweat, I bolted up into a sitting position and focused on my tweed window shade. Something had unlocked that mental vault in my sleep, and I remembered everything.

Everything.

"Oh my God." My words sounded like gunshots in my quiet room.

I replayed every scene, from walking out of the restaurant, to Charles approaching me with a hungry smile after the stranger—the Boss—had left. Charles had stopped right in front of me, his eyes raking down my body. Faster than lightening, he grabbed my head and stared into my eyes. I watched in petrified confusion as his smile slipped. His fluffy eyebrows settled over his eyes like low-lying clouds.

"I can't penetrate," he'd admonished, speaking to the shadow man behind him.

They were real!

"You aren't supposed to touch her," the other had said, releasing Jared. "The Boss will rip you apart if you defy a direct order."

Jared stared straight ahead, his eyes glazed and unseeing. He looked like a robot powering down.

"I can't wipe her memory." Charles had leaned closer to me, searching my eyes for a clue to solve his puzzle.

"Some humans are extraordinarily dimwitted. Here, I'll help."

I'd had time to feel indignation before my mind went blank.

What had we stumbled upon? They'd called us humans. Somehow, they'd used their minds to assert their will.

It sounded like a fable.

That same damned trickle of adrenaline I always got when riding in a really fast car had my heart hammering and my energy zinging. My whole world was topsy-turvy, but one thing was clear.

I had to see him again. I had to see the Boss.

I needed to know what was going on. Was I losing my mind? Were the mushrooms on my steak the funny kind that made me see things? Did I ingest some Ecstasy without knowing it? Because Jared had been right: only drugs could explain last night. It was the only plausible reason for what I was sure transpired.

I slowly lowered my head to the pillow, eyes trying to bore a hole through my window shade. What I had sensed earlier was no longer there. The Boss was gone.

I still had no idea how I knew, only that it felt like something was missing. Something I longed for.

As the next evening fell, I was in street clothes and running shoes. It had not escaped me that I was doing something so stupid it was life-threatening. At the very least I was heading to a bad neighborhood. Even if I didn't find man-shaped shadows, and even if I didn't prove that what I'd experienced was real, if not completely outlandish, I was still heading toward a pack of dangerous homeless hoodlums. There was a reason people on that side of town steered clear of shelters and church-goers offering help. Even wearing grubby black clothes, I still looked like a spoiled brat from a middle-classed family.

God, I was stupid. But I had to know.

Some part of me thought only these shadow men would know why I was different. They might be able to shed a glimmer of light on why I noticed them and others didn't. Why my memory was returned to me, and not Jared, who was still a clueless, humping mess.

I stepped out into the night, a strange new world now that I suspected what the darkness harvested. I peered into each shadow I passed, and even scanned under my car for hidden villains. I imagined the headlights of my old, dilapidated Firebird scurrying strange critters out of my way.

"I should go home." My voice echoed in the quiet car. "I should turn around, right now, and go home."

A second later I was walking at a fast pace toward last's night's episode with my hood over my head and my hands in my pockets. I'd have to work on self-control another time. A man to my right took a blanket from his shopping cart, his smell churning my stomach as I hurried past. Another man, ten feet down the sidewalk, was lighting a cigarette, the flame flickering light across his focused brow. Eyes the color and cloudiness of smoke peered upwards, noticing me.

I hurried on, now approaching the alley where I knew we'd stood. I recognized the shamble of a broken chair and the sparse remnants of a car window sprinkled over the curb. The alleyway was empty.

Damn!

"Hey pretty lady."

A man in a tattered coat stood behind me at an awkward lean. His pants were baggy and tied to his waist with a frayed rope.

"What you lookin' for way over here? You needin' a good time?" The man stepped closer, his face obscured by a matted brown beard.

Fear stabbed my chest. This was one of the many reasons why I shouldn't have come.

I cleared my throat and raised my chin, fingering the whistle in my pocket.

Yes, that was the only weapon I could procure. A stinkin' rape whistle. I wasn't batting a thousand in the preparedness department. It was like all the craziness from my recent experience warped my logic, and now I was just flying by the seat of my pants. I should be outraged at the treatment of Jared and me, and scared of what lurked in the shadows—instead, I just had three times as many questions. My brain couldn't wrap around everything going on, so it stuck to what I could control, and waited for answers.

Right now, though, I needed to get out of here or things would get a whole lot worse.

"I was just leaving." I turned quickly and headed back the way I'd come, only to realize I'd been followed.

Two men blocked the sidewalk, dressed similar to the man stepping to my back.

This was very bad news.

Before I could run, or even get my whistle to my mouth, rough hands took hold of my shoulders and jostled me, my body crashing against the stone wall. He was on me a moment later, his smell making me retch, his hands fumbling at my breasts.

I screamed, fighting him, trying to bat his hands away and get my knee in a position to crush his balls. His hand came up, poised, ready to strike my face. I had one second to feel an all-consuming terror, a crawling sensation dominating my panic-stricken thoughts, before suddenly his whole body was ripped away, thrown to the side like he was made of rags.

The man's head *thunked* against the side of the alley before his body slid to the ground.

I looked up with wild eyes.

In front of me was the stranger. The Boss. Six-and-a-half feet of lethal muscle, poised over me possessively. He turned his broad shoulders toward the two men cornering me. Everyone scattered.

Literally.

As if an invisible shock wave of fear washed over the street, everybody in sight fled. Some men hobbling, some moving in jerky thrusts of knees, some with the speed only PCP could lend, they all took off. One man didn't even bother to buckle his britches. His lady love in tow, street weathered and down-trodden, wiping her mouth as she galloped after him.

I turned back to the giant in front of me, eyes wide, fear still pinging through my body.

"You aren't real bright, even for a human."

I saw him more clearly now than I ever had. He had a chiseled face with high cheek bones and a straight nose. His strong jaw lent him a heavy dose of masculinity, but his long lashes and dark eyebrows softened him into something out of a magazine. The effect was stunning.

My whole body bowed in a huge sigh of relief. *Safety.* "Thank God you showed up."

"Why are you here?"

I held up my palm and shook my head. "Wait. Just... wait." I took a few steps away. "I thought I was going to get raped. God, that was stupid!" With hands on hips, I took a few big, lung-filling breaths. When the bursts of fear completely subsided, I strolled back to my previous position, looking up at the holder of, hopefully, many answers.

As I met his black eyes, his puzzled expression deepened. "You're human…"

"We established that, yes. What I want to know is, if I am human, what does that make you? And why do I notice you when others usually don't?"

His head cocked to the side. His easy balance, his lethal edge; he was like a blade resting on billowing silk. "Very few humans are able to withstand our pheromones. Fewer still to break a *Kolma* once it has been placed. You've not been trained, that's obvious; so how is this possible when you're definitely human? Do you possess the blood of another species?"

I could barely think past the pounding ache of my body, begging to touch him. I needed to get a grip! He was revealing some very interesting factoids I needed to jot down in my mental notebook.

His nostrils flared. "Charles was right; your arousal is a unique scent. Like a spicy, warm drink on a mid-winter's night. It rises above other smells, entrancing the mind."

"Umm," charged with questions, determination, anger, and demands, I thrust forward, "Listen, what did you mean about withstanding the…pher-thing? Or breaking the other thing? How can you trap someone's head with pleasure? Because I'm pretty sure—not positive, but pretty sure—that Jared is straight. And also, I really think we should circle back to what the hell you are, and why nobody knows that you exist? Because this whole people scattering thing is not normal, and I think an explanation is probably in order."

He stepped closer, not hearing me, or not caring that I spoke. His eyes looked at me like I was a life-sized riddle. They delved, searching. He took another step, forcing me to retreat two steps to keep distance between our bodies. Another step back had my back to the wall.

A small smile curved his lips. "I exude pleasure, you run. I exude fear, you come calling. You want me, I can smell it. I can feel it, almost like a palpable thing. Give in to it. Yield to me."

Oh God I wanted to. His body was mere inches from mine, his intense eyes looking down into my soul from a face out of a Renaissance painting. The power of him, the sheer strength, had strange, primal fantasies running amok through my head. My core tingled, my chest surged, and my nipples were so hard they could cut this stone wall.

Why had I come here, again?

He bent, sucking in a big breath through his nose. His face dipped to my neck, hot breath soaking into my fevered skin. A large hand landed on the swell of my hip, firm and in control.

"Nu-uh." I pushed at him, unable to help my sigh. His leg slid in-between my thighs, pressing up against my core, applying warm heat to an area sodden with desire. My hands fell to my sides weakly as his tongue flicked out, tasting my hot skin. He moaned, a deep sound resonating from the base of him, licking down my body like a tongue.

"That's right." His mouth lightly sucked at the base of my neck. Lingering on my pulse. A scrape of tooth had me moaning, honing in on his fingers as they lightly grazed my skin.

"Shouldn't," I muttered, my eyes fluttering as his fingertips trailed over my body. His groin was moving against me in slow, rhythmic thrusts, unhurried and self-assured I would submit. "Can't."

His mouth glanced across my chin then up to my lips. As his full lips touched mine, my thoughts started to swirl. He tasted like wild wine and spice—decadent heaven. His tongue entered my mouth in needful thrusts, expertly playful and sexy at the same time. His bulge was hitting my sweet spot, turning my body into liquid fire.

Logic screamed at me to push away. To get away from this.

But I had never felt like this before. Never been touched like this.

I'd never had the pounding of my heart echoed in another, almost as if they were two halves of a whole. As if I finally fit somewhere; a niche where I'd always belonged, I just hadn't found until right now. Every ounce of my being begged to give in; to submit to him totally.

Then the fire and crazy thoughts started to frost over, starting with my throat and working down the meat of my body. My bones felt like they were turning brittle. Lust was replaced with a tingling of warning, pricks of ice cold pain.

This wasn't the logical side of my brain, it was something else. A warning.

I put a tentative hand to his shoulder, stilling his movements.

Suddenly he was off me, air replacing his scorching body. He whirled, leather duster billowing out behind him. A gleaming, curved sword blossomed in his hand out of nowhere, the other hand twirling a knife.

"What the hell?"

Chapter Five

Freezing cold cracked my bones as my fingers and toes were taken over with frost bite. A pressure filled the air, condensing around me, pushing me back against the wall.

In the middle of the street, like a heat wave taking form, materialized two shapes. They were like disproportioned humans with a monster-like flare. The one on the left had grotesque, burly shoulders. Its arms were stringy, like exposed muscle. Its legs were similar, each limb ending in long, three inch claws. A head like a bull, it had no eyes, just a large, gaping mouth filled with two rows of sharp teeth.

Next to it was a taller shape, like a man made of leather. Its face was an oval, completely smooth; the only feature were two glowing, green orbs posing as eyes. Its hands and feet also ended in claws.

What was truly strange was not the monster-like quality, but the fact that as they stood, they threw off an aura of darkness. It wasn't like the Boss, who cloaked himself in shadow—these suffocated light, killing it until hope turned into despair. It was like an endless night, knowing you'd never be greeted by the sun again.

I huddled against the wall, too terrified to run, not sure what they were, or what they wanted, but knowing the thread connecting me to life was a meager thread indeed if they came after me.

The one with the bull head stepped forward, long claws flexing, its gaping mouth opening wider. The maw issued forth a swarm of insects in a plumb, the buzz nearly deafening my ears. Five foot by five, the giant cloud rocketed out from its body, heading straight for the Boss, who stood protectively in front of me.

He surged forward, meeting the plumb with swinging sword, the blade glowing a burnished gold. It sliced through the insect hoard like a stick through sand, cutting a path that immediately turned into wisps of smoke. Sword moving in a figure eight, over and over, the Boss was pushed back, struggling with the hoard as if it was a solid unit instead of thousands of small insects clustered together.

The Leather-Man-Monster sprung upwards, a huge arc flying through the air. The creature caught and sucked in the light, a streak of darkness slicing through the glow of the distant streetlight. It landed with a soft *squelch*, claws sinking into the Boss's flesh.

It was here I could play hero and save the day. Deep in my bones I knew I could stop this. I could banish these things, rip them from the Boss's back and ground them to paste.

I also knew those thoughts were illusions of grandeur, because if a giant man with a sword couldn't handle this mess, what the hell could a small woman with a rape whistle do?

So I watched in horror as the Leather Man slid down the Boss's back, leaving scores deep in the leather coat. The Boss thrashed, having cut through the insect hoard, and now reaching back with his gold bladed dagger, slicing the left leg of the lithe monster.

With a screech that made my teeth grind, the Leather Man convulsed, half its leg falling, turning to wisps of smoke before it hit the ground. The rest of its body flew skyward, hovering for the briefest of moments like Spiderman as gravity grabbed hold, then landing five feet away, claws outstretched. The now-lopsided creature teetered before falling to the ground. It was enough time for the Boss to shrug out of his shredded leather duster, revealing a leather vest underneath with six gaping tears, red oozing out.

Vivid blue tattoos circled his arms like serpents, before flashing a burnished gold along his skin. He crouched, coiled, and sprung all in one elegant, oiled movement. He slashed at the struggling Leather Man creature, his blade slicing a diagonal line through its chest.

The high-pitched scream echoed again, making me clamp my hands over my ears. A red slash burnt across the Leather Man's middle, tendrils of smoke rising where the sword had passed through.

The Boss, not resting, plunged his knife downward, business end stabbing through the creature's head. It started to shake violently, but I couldn't let my eyes remain. A strange chanting penetrated my awareness.

Still huddling on the ground, I stared at the bull creature. It was making foreign sounds; strange guttural incantations with a peculiar tongue lilt. It certainly wasn't English, and it definitely was dangerous.

As that last thought tumbled through my head, a blue cloud rolled and boiled around it, almost like an aura encompassing its chest and head. The blue cloud, like a heavily pregnant stomach with an active baby, gave the impression of shapes moving within.

"Where are they?" the Boss spat, turning from a strange puddle in the street, like tar with a metallic surface. His eyes swept toward me. "Run Sasha! I won't let it follow you. You'll be safe. I'll find you after."

I couldn't tear my eyes away from the remaining monster.

I could feel that pulsing blue cloud, as if it fanned a spark deep within. It sang to me, hinting at wonders so divine a mortal would be hard-pressed to live after experiencing them. Wouldn't want to. Wouldn't want to exist in a life devoid of the power and majesty within that blue cloud.

I felt my heart reach out, as if extending from my chest. My body started to flush, then heat, prickles sticking my arms, my chest and my head— just like acupuncture—and awakening my senses. Something in my middle blossomed, expanding outward until my skin felt stretched over it. I wanted to laugh so hard, my face cracked and my teeth loosened. I wanted to jump so high, I sailed over God; dance so hard, I broke a hip.

The liquid pulsed and heaved, gaining momentum, but weakly. I had no idea how I knew, but it held only a trickle of power. A card house outdoors; all one needed was a light breeze.

I didn't know how to blow.

The Boss ran at it, slashing. My eyes hadn't left the monster.

The bull beast had stepped out from behind its creation. The flow of power stopped and tied, allowing the creator to move freely, leaving its creation to carry out its duty. The bull beast was headed my way.

"Oh God, oh God, oh God." My voice sounded frail and weak, a poor representation of the budding strength within my chest.

The bull beast stepped up onto the curb, its eyeless face pointed at me. It was expectant. Hungry. Its clawed fingers were moving excitedly, talons clicking together as it approached.

"*Run* Sasha!" the Boss shouted.

Reality snapped like a ruler against the inside of a wrist. *Run!*

"I can offer you great rewards." Words came out in a garbled cluster of syllables, but I understood it. Its power pulsed. Reaching for me.

Something within my chest tried to reach back.

"Oh crap!"

I feinted right like a boxer and bolted left, running smack into an immovable object. I ricocheted off and flew head over heels into a pile of rotted crates, my foot falling through a stack of three and getting stuck at the bottom. "Oh no!" I cried in panic, trying to shake my foot free with a hand on the slimy wall for balance.

A giant man was standing in my path, sword drawn, red-orange blade. The tip swung backward before it slashed down, nearly poking my eye. I hunkered down, leg forgotten, just trying to not get killed by friendly fire.

Glowing blade slashed again. The dance of warfare took the giant guy throughout the alley, slicing off pieces of the monster one at a time. Another shape rushed in, huge and bulky, just like the others.

With three against one, plus a weird blue creation, the fight was over in less time than it took me to realize my trapped foot was in a puddle of sludge currently soaking into my sock. Yanking it free, losing some skin off my ankle in the effort, I finally looked up. Then cowered again.

The three mountainous men were staring at me in semi-circle, swords loosely at their sides. The blades were all silver again, making me wonder if they were actually light sabers and this was all an elaborate joke on the human.

"Her again, Boss?"

I recognized that striking face. Charles. The third addition to this group was unfamiliar, with a mild case of the handsome disease and the same overbearing, yet mouth-watering body.

"Yes." The Boss's tone was curt and his chest puffed slightly, trying to bend his shoulder blades back to ease the tension on the middle of his back.

"Can we keep her?" Charles persisted.

"He's hurt." I pointed at the Boss.

It didn't shake Charles's single-minded focus.

"How bad?" said the third addition, speaking in a harmonious, mid-range voice that probably lent extremely well to singing.

"It's nothing. Take her to her car and see her home. Do not touch her." The Boss's eyes, brimming with the assurance of authority, gripped Charles for a moment, making sure his command was understood. Then he turned to me and said, "Let him get you home safely."

Charles said, "I did last time, didn't I? I can be trusted with your pets." Charles almost sounded sulky. He suddenly seemed a lot younger than he looked.

The Boss nodded once, swept a glance past me, and turned away, crimson oozing down the black leather covering his back. The Singer followed, not bothering with a glance in my direction. Charles hovered.

"I would send you away, but then I'd probably get mugged and killed," I said, stepping out of the alley, my left foot sloshing within my shoe. Like Jared the day before, my brain was on vacation. Again.

"Yesterday you smelled so great. Today you smell like dead rat. What gives?" Charles stepped beside me, taking the street-side of the sidewalk as we ambled back toward my car.

"Don't talk to me. You tried to force me!" I shivered.

"Hey! That wasn't my fault! I've only met a few humans. Usually they're all gung-ho. How was I supposed to know you didn't want me? Obviously you're the problem here, not me—all the chicks dig me."

I scoffed at him. "*Really?* Can you be any more of an egotistical jackass?"

"Sure, if you want. I thought you weren't into that sorta thing, though."

I gave up. The man was dense. Or else really young despite his appearance. There was no other explanation.

"What are you guys?" I sidetracked. "What were those things? Why did the one make a blue…thing? Why do your swords glow? Am I going crazy? What's happening to me?"

Charles whistled as I wound down to a stop. He clasped his hands behind his back in a thinking pose. It was probably a fruitless effort. "The first three would take too long to explain, and we'd probably just wipe the memories from your head anyway, making any explanation wasted time. And if I have extra time, I like to spew batter, not chatter."

"Gross," I muttered, spotting my car up ahead.

"As for the other questions—well, you aren't *going* crazy, but possibly have been for some time. And nothing, yet, but if you'd care to remove your clothes, I will *happen* to you at least twice, quick or slow, hard or soft—entirely up to you."

I ignored him. Suddenly I was bone weary. My limbs felt like they weighed a hundred pounds each.

"Firebird, huh? Old school. My kinda girl."

I sighed hugely. "It goes fast. Look, thanks for the—what are you doing?"

Charles stopped halfway to stuffing himself into my passenger seat. One eyebrow quirked as his lips tugged down at the corners. "Sitting? What do you mean? Is that a weird, human trick-question? I'm confused."

"Why are you getting in my car? Get out."

His mouth fell into a full frown. "The Boss gave a command—how are you resisting? You're human."

"Yeah, so you people—or whatever—keep reminding me. Look, I don't need an escort. I've got plenty of gas, my...don't you sit all the way down or...don't you shut that...*damn it!*"

I fell into the seat with my finger already out. "Get out. Seriously."

"This will go a lot faster if you just drive. You're too small to make me do anything I don't want to do. And just small enough to make me do anything you say as long as you—"

"Take off my clothes, I know." I sighed and started the car. It would almost be easier just to give in.

I rode to my apartment in sulky silence, which didn't prevent Charles from gabbing merrily about a whole lot of absolutely nothing. He sounded like a boy barely on the man side of puberty. If I didn't need my hands to steer, I would have had a finger stuffed as far in my ears as possible.

I parked in the space designated for my apartment, waited for the monstrous man to unfold from the confines of my car, and beeped the alarm on. I turned toward home, so tired I could barely stand, needing sugar to cure the adrenaline crash and possible shock I was enduring.

"Wait, one thing."

I turned back. "What now?"

He surprised me with his proximity. Before I could blink, his hand was on my head.

I awoke with a groggy head sometime in the mid-morning. I lay on top of the covers in my bed, wearing a black hoodie and dirty, spotted jeans. My left shoe was covered in a vile smelling brown sludge, as was my comforter under my foot.

I labored to sit up, moving a hand up to my fuzzy head. I felt like I'd been drinking.

I thought back to the night before. Then blinked in confusion. I couldn't remember. Not last night, and not even the majority of yesterday. It was like huge pieces of my memory were wiped clean.

Sighing, struggling to remember what day it was, I stared at my calendar, and then checked my clock. Red numbers read 7:35.

Why couldn't I remember yesterday? Did Jared drug me for kicks or something?

A memory fluttered at the edge of consciousness. I grasped at it, catching nothing but stale air. My eyes glanced over my room, finding my purse on the ground by the door.

I never put my purse on the ground. I always put it on a chair or counter top to keep the bottom clean. I'm anal like that.

After a few moments of staring at it like a hog looking at a wristwatch, I lay back down and closed my eyes. I would skip first period.

Chapter Six

"Hey, whaddya doing?" Charles stepped forward with Jonas toward the apartment complex, reaching a hand out to stop his brother-at-arms. "We're just supposed to watch and make sure he doesn't go wandering around. We're not supposed to go in."

"The Boss doesn't care about this weasel. He only cares about the girl. Let's have some fun."

"Okay, but, the girl likes this guy, so the Boss wants this guy safe."

"He'll be plenty safe. I'll take him to Third Three. He'll be fine. Time of his life." Jonas waited beside the door until a human, so unobservant it might as well have been blind, unlocked the apartment complex door and went through, completely missing their presence. Jonas stepped forward in a smooth, quick glide, catching the door before it clicked into its bed.

"This just isn't a good idea," Charles whined, following.

Jonas often pushed the envelope. His tastes generally bent toward pain, liking when his victims screamed and begged for their life. It wasn't a perversion, per se, since being a hunter was in their genetic makeup, but it wasn't exactly normal, either. The majority of their species leaned more toward wanton pleasure any way they could get it, with any one they could get it, pushed higher and harder with another willing participant. Oh sure, there were the dominance games, which could be fun, but all-in-all everyone was in it for a good time.

It was why Charles was supposed to keep an eye on Jonas—make sure he didn't do anything stupid. Terrible idea, obviously. Jonas was one of the best they had, brutal without mercy and extremely effective. Charles was an up-and-comer with a lot of potential.

Which meant he'd get his ass kicked if he got in Jonas's way.

They made it silently up two flights of stairs and down the hall without anyone noticing. As Jonas waited outside the human's door, he snickered. "It's almost too easy. These humans don't notice nothing."

"That's because they don't want to know what goes bump in the night when they're safely behind their alarms and locks. That girl human does, though. She peeks right into the shadows and picks us out, remember? What's with that? It creeps me out. We're supposed to be the dominant species…"

"Shut up, I can hear him coming. I don't want him to scream before I can Dose him. That'll just get messy."

Jonas knocked quietly. They heard three footsteps before the door swung open, a chubby male with a shock of orange hair holding a candy bar staring at them with round eyes. "Hello?"

"Who are you?" Jonas asked in a low voice, stepping into the small apartment. Charles followed quickly, scanning the corridor to make sure they weren't seen.

"Whu—" The male's face went slack.

"That worked fast," Charles noticed, eyes dipping to this fellow's stiffening dick. "He's dim-witted, then? Is that why he succumbed so fast?"

Jonas stepped around the human male and walked to the back of the apartment in quick, smooth strides. "Some just have less defense against it. Doesn't have much to do with their I.Q. Some of the dumb ones can really give you problems."

"Oh." Charles stepped away from the kid's groping hands. "No thanks, bro, you're not my type. Sorry. We didn't know anyone else was home."

Jonas stepped out from the bedroom at the back of a frumpy apartment. "He's not in his room."

"Human male," Charles spoke to the kid, and then danced away from outstretched arms, "where's your friend?"

"Roommate!" Jonas yelled, stepping beside the male.

The kid turned to Jonas with huge eyes, his hands falling to his side. He started to tremble.

"Now, Jonas, bro, this isn't the time for screaming," Charles lectured. "You know what the Boss said; we're supposed to keep a low profile tonight."

"You nag." Jonas tugged down his zipper, letting his pheromones change back to lustful coaxing. "Suck it in, Carrot Top, I ain't got all day."

"Jonas, Jesus—can't you do that before we go out? We have stuff to do tonight." Charles blew out a breath in impatience.

"Takes the edge off. Besides, these humans think they're the masters of the universe. It's good for them to know someone bigger is lurking around."

The door handle of the front door jiggled just as Charles was about to complain again. The knob turned, revealing the tall, thin Jared they'd met a couple days ago.

"What the—?" Jared froze, stunned.

"Howdy partner, good to see ya again. Let's go ahead and invite you inside, huh?" Charles ushered him in, hitting him with a good Dose of pheromones to loosen him up. Human males had the propensity to scream with their first experiences with other men. They really needed to relax and just let the good times happen.

Which was exactly what Charles was helping him do with the Dose.

"What's happening?" Jared stared down at his roommate.

Charles sighed, impatiently staring at Jonas. "C'mon, bro. Hurry this along. I'm getting a weird feeling we're going to get caught."

"The Boss is on the other side of the city. He's dealing with a turf breach. We're good. I'm… almost…" Jonas flexed.

Charles noticed two slim hands reaching for his crotch. He slapped them away and stepped toward the door. "I'm not in the mood, kid. Jonas, handle this guy, would ya?"

Breathless for a moment but not inactive, Jonas zipped up, and then stepped forward and slipped a bag over Jared's head. Before Charles could protest, Jonas had the kid's hands bound behind his back and over a shoulder.

As they walked out the door, Charles asked, "Aren't you going to mind wipe Carrot Top?"

"No time. We got what we came for, now we gotta go."

All Charles could do was shake his head. He had a really bad feeling about all this.

Chapter Seven

"Damn it!" I sat forward in the still room, silence wrapping me in a thick blanket. A moment of contemplation had me catapulting out of my bed and into some sweats. It was just after ten at night and I knew Jared would still be up.

"Think they can just keep sucking my brain out of my head, do they?" I jerked my hood over my head. "Well, joke's on them—just like school, it doesn't stick!"

I slipped into my tennis shoes and snatched my handbag. "I am going to give them a piece of my mind! Just as soon as I make sure Jared isn't in some weird orgy!"

Just like the last time I spent a whole day with no recollection as to what happened the night before, I awoke remembering everything. Only this time, the recall was faster. It was as if my brain remembered the path out, and took it just as soon as my consciousness got out of the way.

I hesitated at the door for a brief second…then shrugged and grabbed my rape whistle off the table by the door. You just never knew.

I really needed to get a proper weapon…

Fifteen minutes later and I was knocking on Jared's apartment door. It opened with a swirl of desperation, his red-headed roommate looking out at me, butt-ass naked.

"Uh…" I cleared my throat and stepped backward. "What, uh…what's going on, Billy? You, uh…you're naked…"

"I sucked a man's dick!"

I'd been doing a lot of confused blinking in the last couple of days, and this was no exception. "That's something. Is, uh, is Jared here?"

"Did you hear me? Why the fuck did I suck a man's dick, Sasha? Am I gay?" Billy's eyes were wild and unfocused. His cock was standing on end.

Suddenly I knew exactly what happened, and it wasn't very nice to leave his memories intact. Poor Billy was scared out of his head, having known he liked girls his whole life and suddenly unsure; but unlike a drunken night of experimentation, he had been blind-sided. Unfortunately, I didn't know how to talk him down, nor did I want to get any closer. Billy's eyes were starting to lose their focus, sliding down my body in unmasked lust.

"I need to screw you," he said immediately.

I took another step back. "Is Jared in there?"

"Nah, he got kidnapped. C'mon pretty pussy cat, I wanna pet you."

"You need to stay in your house until this wears off, Billy. You're dangerous."

"I'm a thrill ride. Wanna ticket?"

Ugh! I turned and ran down the hall, looking back before I hit the stairs to make sure Billy turned back into his house. Miracle of miracles, thankfully he did.

That wasn't right. Doing that to him wasn't how to treat people. At the same time, killing strange monsters and carrying around swords wasn't normal, either.

Focus on what you can control.

"Kidnapped?" I asked myself, knowing full well it was Charles and that other, scary guy.

Outside his apartment complex I slowed to a walk, thinking. How would I know where they took him? Because I had to get him back—that was a given. I could go back to that alleyway where those guys tended to pop up, but having been accosted by a homeless man, and met by crazy monsters that could spit out other, more colorful monsters, I wasn't in a hurry to go alone.

I sank into the driver's seat of my Firebird. Those guys must live somewhere. They may not be human, apparently, but everything needed a place to reside. So the question then became: Where did they live?

Probably on the bad side of town, since the Boss referred to it as his territory.

Suddenly, in full action, I started my car and stepped on the gas. Some guy dove out of the way, groceries flying.

"Sorry!" I yelled out the window, berating myself for not looking first.

Speeding to my general destination, I couldn't help but feel a hard pang of guilt. In the back of my head I knew, just *knew*, this had to do with my secret box. I'd finally found the things I'd been catching glimpses of my entire life (they were real!), and while a huge part of me was relieved I wasn't crazy, Jared was somewhere right now probably thinking he was. My life had officially started to corrode him.

It was only a matter of time.

Slowing as I neared the old crash site from a couple of nights ago, I noticed the fresh scar on the tree. I kept driving, letting out the other contents of my secret box and grasping a really helpful little tool. I'd always thought of it as women's intuition, just a lot more potent than other people's. I could find a diamond earring on a soccer field after everyone else had looked all day and given up. I had feelings about pop quizzes. I could guess someone's intentions a second before they acted on them. It wasn't failsafe, and it didn't always work, but when it did, miracles happened.

I needed a miracle right now.

In a weird kind of daze, I let my inner voice guide me, my arms dropping to the right on the steering wheel, then the left, taking turns until I slowed in the nicer part of town. Low and behold, looming up on the left, huge and brooding, was a freaking mansion! A fortress, more like, dominating the neighborhood with size and well... weirdness. It had gothic-looking spires and busts, three visible stories, and took up half a block. Oh yeah, and gargoyles huddled along the sweeping roof, snarling out at the street.

How had people not petitioned? How had I not heard of a relic from Ghostbusters? Where was the key master? All good questions for yet another time; I had found the right place.

"Homey," I muttered, taking in the dark brown paint with black trim.

A woman, moving as if made from silk, made her way down the sidewalk and turned onto the path to the front door. She was tall and lithe, beauty showcased in a shimmery, see-through gown.

"Yeah, this is the right place, all right."

When had I taken up talking to myself?

I slipped out of my car silently and bush hopped until I was crouching next to the porch, watching the quiet street in the darkness. I had to assume that the other houses were owned by normal people, and normal people didn't gallivant outside at midnight. That just left me with the non-normal people who were definitely living, or at least residing, in this house.

I glanced at the door, shifting within my bush. I really didn't want to go in and face the crazy. I hadn't forgotten how large those guys had been, or Goddamn strong Charles was. I poked the guy in the eyeball and he just reached out to palm my breast, completely unconcerned! Who was I fooling? What help would I be trying to break Jared out of here?

I should call the cops. That's what I should do. Report a kidnapping.

Except, these non-humans could apparently bend people to their will sexually. I had to imagine that crossed over into just influencing people, period. These people could also somehow hide gothic castles within the city limits. Something told me cops would be ineffective. Plus, I'd been hiding my secrets for so long, I knew better than to stick my neck out.

So, hero it is. Ugh.

Steeling my courage, I tiptoed out of the bush and scurried up the steps, pausing at the door. All was quiet. Fingers tingling, I turned the ornate handle and opened the door a crack, braced with flight in mind.

Silence.

The breath slowly exited my lungs. *Here we go.*

I peeped my head in, eyes scanning furiously for occupants.

My noisy inhale was not in the plans.

It was like I had just stepped into a rich person's house in the early nineteen hundreds. The colors were lush wood and browns with pinky-purple velvet chairs and a marble fireplace. Large rugs adorned the floor and sweeping drapes styled the windows. It was an outer room, made for company and pleasant chatting, and completely clean—no mess, no dishes, and no clutter. If it wasn't for the muted glow from electric lamps, I would've thought I jumped back in time.

Keeping to the sides, I edged my way deep into the room toward the back where there was a nondescript door almost blending into the wall. This was where my inner sense directed me, whispering that Jared lay deep in the heart of this place. He would be in a room with a lot of people, mindlessly held prisoner, entertaining a great many people as they, in turn, entertained him.

My stomach twisted, strengthening my resolve.

I scampered across the spacious room and paused again, turning the handle slowly. Well-oiled hinges, thank God. Another old-timey room waited beyond, but this one was decorated like a study of some kind. A huge rack of books—the term bookcase was too small for this masterpiece—dominated the back wall. A couch and a few chairs were positioned near the middle of the room with a large, mahogany desk sitting against the other wall.

Empty. Still lucky.

I once again scurried through, trying to make absolutely no noise. At the other door, I paused to listen, my palm on the handle. It was here I heard murmuring through the heavy wood door. *Crap!*

I bounced around like a spider, trying to figure out where to go. The voices got louder—*they're coming this way!*

My eyes dusted the sizable space, lingering on the desk. A few quick steps had me swiping a vicious-looking letter opener. It wasn't a gun, but it was much more effective than a whistle.

Except they had huge swords.

I stuffed the pointy object in my pocket anyway—hopefully that didn't come back to bite me if I fell—and thought about running toward the other door. Except they'd just follow me. Then where would I go, back to that bush? Counter-productive.

I closed my eyes, feeling that intuition pointing toward the wall behind the desk. I was there a second later, poking and prodding the thing, dancing like a child that had to pee, trying to figure out if it opened or my secret box was screwing with me.

"I don't know why Jonas has a sudden vendetta against the human. Did the Boss call him down, I wonder?" A woman inquired as the door opened a crack.

Oh holy crap!

I dove beneath the desk, bumping the chair out of the way, and tried to control my panting.

Two pairs of feet entered the room, a person with spikey red heels and black fishnet stockings, and a man with shiny black shoes and slacks. I could only see up to about their knees.

"It is always wise to either compliment, or ignore, items that Jonas finds interesting. He is not a male to trifle with." The man was headed through the room, the woman on the far side from me.

Please don't need to write a letter at this desk...

"Anyway, Jonas isn't the one who concerns me..." the woman purred.

The heels stepped in front of the shiny shoes so their toes were almost touching. I heard a wet kiss, then the guy was shifting on his feet—he marginally spread his legs.

Seriously? Did these people ever do anything else besides fight and have sex?

"Well, darling, I must leave you. We can finish this another time. I have a million things to do for the Boss and you know how I hate to keep him waiting."

"Let's be quick."

The feet danced, one red heel stepping to the side of the man's legs, one flying skyward and disappearing.

The sounds of kissing resumed, the feet starting to rock.

"One quick one before I leave, then," the man murmured.

I nearly groaned in frustration.

The other heel disappeared as shimmery red fabric pooled onto the floor. The shiny black shoes took a few quick steps away from me, two clothed butts landing on the couch in my line of sight. Fingers wearing red polish to match the shoes scrabbled at the man's zipper, peeling his pants away to the side eagerly. I squeezed my eyes shut again, wanting to hum in order to drown out the moans and heavy breathing.

"Lick me, Rupert," the woman purred.

I peeked an eye open in gross fascination, seeing a man's hand rub down the woman's thigh and across her panty-covered sex. His fingers rubbed up and down the middle, scratching at her clit, making her moan and gyrate her hips up to him.

"I hope you aren't too partial to these tights," he said in a low, husky voice. With two hands, he ripped the tights parting in her crease. His fingers snaked under the edge of the red panties— the woman knew how to match her accessories— and stripped the material away. He bent to her glistening sex immediately, licking up the center with a greedy tongue.

"Oh Rupert, *yes!*" she sighed, pushing her hips into his face.

I couldn't look away. They had so much passion and fire, desperate for each other. It was strangely arousing watching it happen.

So great, now I could add peeping Tom to my list of accolades.

"Mmmmm," the man moaned, climbing up her body. He grabbed his sizable erection at the base and threaded it into her.

"*Oh* yes!" The woman moaned, gripping his body with her legs.

Squeezing my eyes shut didn't stop me from hearing the rhythmic squeaking of the couch, his thrusts punctuated by a wet slide and springs shifting. His panting got more labored, pounding into her. She received him with clinging legs and throaty moans.

"Yes!" the man exclaimed, the couch creaking wildly, skin smacking skin.

"Oh, yes, yes, yes!" she exalted as the rocking began to simmer down.

She totally faked it!

Oh God, could Jared tell all those times?

Maybe not, because this guy didn't seem to notice. Or maybe he didn't care. He climbed off when he'd finished and buckled up his pants.

"I'll see you soon," he said while getting his breath.

"Don't you want to share your blood…" she asked hopefully.

My mind stuttered, listening harder, trying to verify what I thought I'd just heard…

"You have a house full of partners, I must leave you to them. Try the human. He must be good for something."

"But none are as powerful as you." She rose from the couch to stop his retreat.

"I must go. I've tarried too long."

He was away a moment later.

In a fit of temper, she stamped her expensive shoe and bent to scoop up her dress. For a brief moment we could've met eyes. Had she looked to her right, she would've found me staring like a mouse hiding from a snake behind a leaf. Dumb, basically.

Luckily, she couldn't smell whatever the men did, and she wasn't under the impression people skulked around and hid under desks. She started walking back the way she'd come. As the door opened, the unmistakable sounds of chatter drifted out and filled the room, only cut off when the heavy wood door was closed once again.

So going that way wasn't an option. Crap.

I crawled from the desk and stared back at the oil painting. My inner compass said go through there. Unlike Mary Poppins, however, I didn't have Dick Van Dyke with his terrible accent to help me jump in.

Sighing in frustration, I held up my hands, feeling for air. Nothing. I felt along the frame for bumps or something, *anything.* It was here, I felt something. An inner twitch maybe, but my fingers stalled halfway down the gilded frame.

I heard more muffled voices through the door. *Hurry!*

Chapter Eight

I leaned closer to the tarnished metal, only then seeing two hairline cracks. Hearing the door handle jiggle, I stuffed my fingers into the space between the metal and canvas and yanked, lifting the metal an inch as if it was on a hinge. A loud pop echoed in the room, the left side of the picture pushed out farther than the right side. A crack formed in the wall under the frame, indicating that it was, indeed, a doorway.

A muffled voice drifted through the door. "I might go find a human of my own for the night. I'd forgotten what fun they can be. Plus, I could use a little drinkie."

The far door was opening, but I didn't want to wait. I struggled with the weight of the secret door, slipped through, and pulled it shut with the gleaming handle on the back. It closed with a soft click, cutting off another man saying, "Let's share one—"

These people—or whatever the hell they were—had an absentee view on morals!

I turned into the room and blinked. It wasn't from confusion this time. It was pitch black. I couldn't see *anything*; not even my hand in front of my face. Not even my hand touching my face!

"Not good," I whispered, just to have something to focus on.

I took a big breath, preventing myself from groping blindly. Partly I was scared what my hands would touch, and partly I'd look a fool, and had a sneaking suspicion that whatever these beings were, they could see a lot better than me in the dark. You don't have shadow clinging to you when you move just to have a hard time navigating the night...

Closing my eyes so the darkness felt like a choice, I focused on that feeling in my chest, looking for guidance from my female intuition. The heat pulsed and throbbed, opening up like a flower and spreading out, making my skin feel tightly stretched trying to contain it.

Opening my eyes again, the medium-sized, rectangular room before me burst into life. Colors of the rainbow swirled and flexed around me, running through the walls and along the ground. In the middle of the room crouched two couches, defined by the absence of color within that space. I noticed a few other pieces of furniture, like tables and a chair or two, also identified by a black hole, but if I wasn't hallucinating, the room seemed pretty bare.

At the end of the square space to the right was a corridor. My feet were moving straight ahead before my mind caught up with it. I crossed the room with easy strides, dipped into the corridor and started jogging down what must be the middle of the fortress-house.

Before I got far, though, a strange feeling nudged me. I'd just passed through the Boss's secret room, I was sure of it. Just like I could sense when that nosey bugger waited outside my apartment, I just *knew.* And something—the same sixth sense that led me to this house—told me I needed to leave my mark. He needed to know without a doubt that it was me. When that voice spoke, I listened, end of story.

The only problem was, there was only one way that he'd be sure, without a doubt, who passed through.

"I cannot believe I am even contemplating this!"

I went to one of the plush couches that my butt identified as leather, laid down, and paused.

"No. Just…no."

As I moved to get up, a surge of doubt washed over me. I had to leave a mark. He had to know. Why? I had no idea. But I knew he did.

"Damn you, inner compass," I whispered, settling back down.

"What has my life become when I'm in a stranger's room, about to—"

I didn't bother finishing that thought. My hand snuck into my britches. I could feel my face burning in embarrassment.

Almost unbidden, the image of those people on the couch surfaced. Of his greedy plunges and her writhing body under him. Then the Boss's body and intimidating pressure pushing into me. His hands, coating my body, feeling between my—

"*Holy—*"

I shuddered barely before I'd even begun.

"—crap," I panted. Well, that was pretty painless.

That done, I jumped up and sprinted down the corridor, my inner compass probably laughing its butt off that I actually went through with it.

The walls climbed with colors, throbbing as if they had a heart. Letting that weird sixth sense continue to guide me, stronger now than I could ever remember, I wound my way through the building, ignoring occasional doors to my left or right, until finally my skin was crawling and my butt cheeks tingling. It was my danger sensor.

That aggressive shadow guy was on the other side of the door in front of me, I had no doubt. And he was dangerous. Breathing deeply, I suddenly wondered how smart this was.

And yes, that thought should have occurred to me long before now.

I took stock of the situation—I was about to barge into a scene with a huge, violent guy who wished me harm. He had wanted to hurt me that other night, I could feel it. He wasn't good or just, he was bad news, untrustworthy and vile. But he hadn't hurt Jared. He obviously didn't have morals, but even still, Jared was most likely physically okay.

Plus, how the hell was I going to save him? I wouldn't come out on top in a fist fight, my sword only scared envelopes, and I had no combat experience.

That's when a muffled scream pushed through the wall and pierced my gut.

Never mind. Jared needed help, and this just got real.

I stepped through the door.

Chapter Nine

Jared lay on his back, his expression one of alarm. A naked woman bounced on his hips, a smile curling her lips. Crouched by Jared's head was Aggressive Shadow—I'd never caught his name—holding a knife. A circle of spectators watched the scene, most naked, almost all touching themselves or each other, getting off on what was happening in front of them.

If my vengeance had a smell in contrast to my arousal, these people would've been covering their noses and retching!

I lunged across the room with letter opener in hand before Jared could issue another scream. Without thought, all action, I had the woman's hair clutched tightly in a fist, her neck taxed from pulling her head back, and the "blade" at her throat, for all the world pretending it was a knife.

Everyone froze.

Aggressive Shadow looked up at me in complete surprise.

"What the hell is this, Jonas?" the woman seethed, her body going a worrying type of fluid.

Aggressive Shadow—Jonas—sat back on his haunches, a quizzical smile playing across his face as he analyzed me. "Well, well, how did you get in here?"

"Walked. Which is exactly how I'll be getting out. Get off she-bitch!" I yanked the woman's hair, dragging her off of Jared.

"Why is she not responding to my fear pheromones?" a man with a buzz cut against the wall asked, mystified. "This has never happened before."

"Seriously, can everyone stop stroking their penises? It is rude, strange, and distracting all at the same time! Social etiquette, people," I shouted, staring at Jonas, the "knife" still at the woman's throat.

I had a sinking feeling the woman was humoring me, based on the bored glaze to her eyes.

"Sasha?" Jared struggled to sit up, bleeding from at least twelve shallow gashes on his chest— some looked like nail scratches.

"Oh God, Jared!" I whispered hoarsely.

White hot rage vibrated my body and clouded my vision. Something shook loose in my chest, removing a blockage I hadn't known existed. That same sixth sense I'd been using got a surge of power, sizzling my limbs as it traveled my length, my skin no longer feeling stretched, but now electrified and translucent.

"Did you feel that?" someone asked in a hushed voice.

I didn't pay attention. I could only focus on Jonas as he rose slowly, uncoiling from the ground in a smooth, graceful lengthening of muscles. His face wore a malicious smile, his eyes lit with a manic fire.

"It was not wise, coming here," Jonas said as he took a step closer.

A burst of sweat coated my body as adrenaline surged through my blood.

I flung the woman to the side, stepping away into a crouch, something primal taking over. Letter opener held in my right hand like a knife, I took my whistle out and put it to my lips. I had no idea why.

"Is that a whistle?" someone asked, dumbfounded.

Obviously, no one else knew why, either.

A smile slid up Jonas's face like an oil slick on wet cement. "I wasn't supposed to seek you out, but since you've come to me, I think I might just have a little fun with you."

"Nothing you do with me will be fun." I stepped toward Jared as Jonas circled me, intending that last line to be threatening, and missing the mark somewhat.

"For you," I clarified.

"You are impervious to our pheromones, which means your screams will be heartfelt, and my cock pounding into you won't be welcomed. I wonder if you'll like it anyway."

Bile rose in my throat.

Skin swished as the crowd shifted position, sounding similar to fabric rustling, only much grosser. But at least what Jonas said made them uncomfortable, too.

I did not harbor false illusions that it would matter in the least.

"You'll have to do it bleeding and deaf because you won't get me—"

He rushed me. One minute he was stalking me like a cat stalks a beetle, and the next he was upon me, his movements so fast and powerful, they'd gotten lost in my vision. Heat pulsed within my chest, sending a throb of electricity down my arms, sizzling my skin as I tried to wrestle my wrist away from his tree-trunk arm. He flinched back with a hiss, giving me enough room to stab the strangely crimson glowing blade downward, sticking into his chest. It didn't go far; I wasn't strong and it wasn't sharp.

They didn't take good care of office supplies in this place.

His hand rose to strike me or choke me, but I didn't wait to find out which. I blew for all I was worth, the whistle hollering in his face and echoing into his ears. He flinched again, his head swinging back, his hearing apparently more acute than mine because he acted like I blared a blow horn at the side of his head.

I dodged around his giant body, still blowing the whistle, and launched at Jared. He was sitting up distractedly, fear still on his face, erection amazingly going strong.

"C'mon, Jared, hurry!" I yelled, tugging at his arm and trying to turn my body to face the attack I knew would come shortly.

"I need to screw, Sasha," he whined, breaking down before my eyes in fear and self-loathing.

Guilt shriveled my gut even more, but anger fueled whatever new power coursed through my midsection. I throbbed with it, a weird sort of fire pounding in my head and pulsating down my limbs.

As Jared tried to stand, Jonas was on me again, his face a mask of violent brutality. The game had ended for him when the first gush of blood pumped out of the new hole in his chest.

He grabbed my arm and flung me, his hand once again flinching back from my skin as if burned, but not before I was airborne. I hit the wall with a thud, my head banging painfully, making Jonas sparkle within my vision. I fell to the ground, needing a second for the stars to dissipate.

Before Jonas could pounce on my prone frame, I jumped up as if my legs were made from a pogo-stick and dove for the letter opener that had fallen when my body hit the wall. Crouched once more, dull "knife" at the ready, I squared off, waiting for that blur of movement I knew would come; but this time, I let my sixth sense feel for it.

Sure enough, my warning butt tingle had me moving a fraction of a second before he launched, slipping out of the way then stabbing down, slicing a red gash across his back with my, once again, crimson glowing blade. It was the first time I was happy he was naked.

Jonas howled and rounded on me.

"Can someone stop stroking their damn penis and help me out?" I yelled. "What the hell is wrong with you people? Ever heard of a do-gooder?"

My "knife" strikes were doing no good, and I was tired. Worse, Jonas wasn't. I wouldn't be able to do enough damage to escape before I passed out from fatigue. If one of these yuck-ups would give me a little distracted cover, I could probably salvage the situation.

Unfortunately, no one even so much as slowed in their personal hand-combat.

These freaking people had something seriously wrong with them!

This time, the butt tingle had me staying still, somehow *knowing* Jonas would anticipate my movement to the side. I stabbed, poking another shallow hole in his body, before sprinting across the room.

He caught me by the hair and yanked me back. My upper body fell toward the floor, my legs swept out and useless. Jonas pinned me to the ground with a hand on my throat before flinching back again, shaking the hand and squatting over me, intent to do me harm, but confused why he couldn't.

"Enough."

A spatter of titillated laughter sounded from the peanut gallery. Jonas, his eyes full of hate, straightened up slowly, regret that his retribution was called off. His body bled from three different gashes, but he seemed unperturbed.

On the other hand, my head pounded, my scalp hurt, I was exhausted, my muscles were sore, and, oh yeah, I was freaked out of my face because Jonas wanted to kill me slowly and with much pain.

I'd just made an extremely violent enemy that melted into the night like butter onto hot bread. I had a sickening feeling I'd just waved goodbye to safety.

All eyes turned to the speaker, one of two clothed people in the room, me being the other, standing just inside the invisible door, staring at me with an unreadable expression.

The Boss had followed my trail. I was suddenly glad I had stopped to listen to my inner guide, however gross.

"Jonas," the Boss said, eyes lazily sliding from me to him, "you are on probation and banned from this house and duty. Dismissed."

Jonas flexed, his eyebrows drooping dangerously. He stepped toward the Boss, coiling. It looked like he planned to take out his vengeance on the Boss.

The Boss continued to stare, but did not change his relaxed posture in any way. He seemed unconcerned.

After a tense stare-off, Jonas dropped his eyes and spit—narrowly missing my head—and walked out.

I wanted to go home.

Chapter Ten

"Sit."

I didn't need to be told twice. I sunk into a velvet upholstered couch in a decked out master bedroom. The 1900's Victorian style carried through to this room, with a lovely chandelier twinkling in the middle, electric candles instead of wax, cream painted wood paneling up to the high ceilings, drapes, rugs, and the lot. It was beautiful. I was almost too tired to appreciate it.

The Boss had taken a seat to my right in a chair, his legs up on a footstool and his fingers intertwined on his lap. Since Jared was being stitched up and calmed down somewhere within the house, there wasn't much I could do but wait. I had decided to trade the Boss for answers, mostly because I didn't have much choice, but also because he seemed to think I had leverage.

"How did you find this place?" he asked in a deep, calm voice.

"I thought I got the first question?"

That perfect face beheld me for a second, utterly patient. "Very well."

He was humoring me. I was too tired to be indignant. "What are you?"

"To your kind, I am a fable, for the most part. A myth. A representation of me exists in stories and ballads, in histories, and within popular culture."

I sighed tiredly. "I hate riddles—I can never figure them out. Can you just tell me like you're talking to a five-year-old?"

"You've heard of vampires?"

I scoffed. "You're saying you're a vampire?"

His lips hinted at a smile. "No. Vampires aren't real. I—my species—inspired the stories of vampires. We're not unlike humans, very similar, actually; but yet, we're not of the same race."

I was not following along. "As in…you're from somewhere else?"

"You use race to denote color, religion, difference in appearance, and other unimportant things. When in fact, those are just differences in genes. Not large differences, either. We, on the other hand, use it to denote somewhat…larger alterations to the fundamental principles in genetics. Our heritages, yours and mine, originate from the same place, but along that evolutionary road, there is a fork. We are on one side of that fork, you are on the other."

"What if I don't believe in evolution?"

"Then God wanted a little more diversity. Either that, or He has a sense of humor."

"Oh, He definitely has a sense of humor," I mumbled. I was proof.

"How did you find this place?" he asked.

"Wait, you didn't actually answer the question. So you aren't human, but you're *like* human?"

"Correct."

"What are the differences?"

"That's another question." His eyes twinkled mischievously, giving me a hot flash. "But I'll answer. We, my species, are physically superior. We're larger, faster, stronger, and have more acute senses. Our eyes work better in low light, like a nocturnal predator. Your kind thinks you're hunters—you're incorrect. *We* evolved as hunters. It's the difference between a domestic cat and a lion."

I opened my mouth to ask more questions, especially since it seemed humans got the crappy end of the gene-pool, but he held up a pointer finger. "My turn."

I let my mouth snap shut. Fair was fair.

"How did you find this place?"

I shrugged, relaying the story of my night. As I got further along, the crease in his brow deepened. When my babbling came to an end, the only sound in the room was the ticking of a clock.

I took that as my cue to ask another question. "Why don't people see you guys or notice you?"

"Your boyfriend's roommate had full memory?" he sidetracked.

"Yes—wait! You have to answer mine first!"

"Very well." The crease didn't lighten. "There's more to this world than humans can tolerate while still hanging onto their oblivion. Humans like their experiences to largely fit in a few categories. Another branch of human, our species, gives them trouble to no end. They don't understand us, making them uncomfortable. What humans don't understand, they fear. What they fear, they kill. There was a lot more burnt at the stake than just witches. We've been found and persecuted often in our history. It then becomes necessary *not* to be found."

"But if you're kind of human, why don't you just fight back? Especially if you're stronger or whatever."

"First, let's return to you. How did you know this was the right place?"

I sighed. "I saw a lady looking like a super model wearing a see-through gown walk into the house. You guys have a strange fascination with sex—I connected the dots."

"Only *we* have a strange fascination?" His eyes were twinkling again, looking at me in a knowing way. It was the wrong time for a burst of arousal to drench my panties.

"Since I doubt you care about the answer to that, I won't count that question."

Laughter rumbled out of his muscular chest. "Generous of you."

"Okay, so, why don't you guys just fight back?"

"Another of our traits is a problem with procreation. Humans procreate like a virus. You don't live as long, but you replace yourself multiple times within your life. We're faster and stronger, but not nearly as populace. Plus, we're violent—preferring to tear our enemies apart face-to-face, rather than creating weapons to do it on a massive scale. Even if we could compete with your numbers, we cannot compete with your bombs and other weapons of destruction. Humans have become absolutely ingenious with inventions, many of which are bent on destruction and monitoring. It's best to steer clear."

"Okay, but—"

He held up a hand again. "How did you find my secret chamber?"

I once again told my story, as fast as possible. Part of my mind, the one raised in a protective bubble, couldn't believe what I was hearing. It sounded so far-fetched—surely I would have heard about this. There was a giant mansion in the city, for cripes-sakes. Someone might have said *something* along the way.

The other part of me, however, that had seen shadows moving in the darkness since I could remember, was soaking up every word. I could understand how they could move through the world undetected, since no one had ever believed me when I'd pointed them out. This man had walked through a street light, in public, and stared at me; but Jared, walking right beside me, hadn't noticed him. The part of me that demanded proof had it, which made my brain immediately soften to what the Boss was saying. Plus, though they were larger and muscled, they did look human. Even if they did get noticed, why would anyone think they were anything different than a football player? Or a really pretty, scary chick?

"How do you stay hidden? And why can I see you?" I fired at him as soon as I could.

"I will count that as one." He waited for me to nod impatiently before he went on. "As you've noticed, we each have various abilities offered to us. Most of us can affect humans with our pheromones, inspiring lust, fear, and a few other emotions with fluctuating degrees of effectiveness. Some are better than others, because some are stronger in magic than others. That trait is one that has become invaluable to staying firmly behind the veil of myth."

My brain stuttered on *magic*, but couldn't process until the issue of my, once believed, craziness was put to rest. "But why can I see you?"

"Anyone who looks hard enough, or opens themselves to it, can see us. Like a magic show, if you pay attention, you can find the strings and hidden doors. I assume you're open to it. What I don't understand is why our pheromones don't work with you."

I shrugged. I had no idea, but I was intensely relieved.

He nodded, guessing as much.

I didn't know whose question it was, so I snuck another one in. "Why do people classify you as vampires?"

The Boss smiled. "That's not how they classify us, it's the myth they created on our behalf. Faster, stronger—"

"Beautiful," I blurted.

A smile ghosted his lips as he nodded. I got the impression he was thanking me for the compliment. "My species is not always beautiful, but some are, yes. We also drink blood."

I choked on my spit. "You drink *blood?*"

He smiled, his eyes sparking with hunger. My body cultivated a similar spark in response.

"There is much power in blood," he explained, his eyes on me steadily, as if I were prey. "Some people have more than others, making them taste sweeter. Like chocolate, or candy. It's better with arousal. Better still if we don't pollute them with pheromones during the extraction. Though that's much more work. Too much, usually, as I have previously explained."

"That's a lovely way of saying it— extraction."

His smile got bigger.

"So you only, uh, drink the blood of humans?"

He closed his eyes and said, "Hmmm. It's amazing that your smell constantly changes. Is it based on your level of arousal, I wonder?" His dark eyes flashed open, analyzing me.

I flushed within that stare, the tug becoming ten times more pronounced. It felt like my body woke up—all the tired and achiness from earlier evaporating, leaving me clearheaded and exuberant. My skin started to tingle and I broke out in goose bumps, wanting to touch him so badly my fingers trembled.

"I have a boyfriend!" I proclaimed abstractly, struggling to regain control.

His eyes never wavered. "Humans are peculiar when it comes to mating. Although, that's probably necessary with a species that procreates so excessively that diseases have bloomed into existence to hinder the ability."

"Right, yes. Uh..." I nearly banged on my head to get it back in gear. His gaze was doing strange things to my stomach. "So you don't take each other's blood? Your own, uh, kind I mean?"

"As I said, within blood is power. Humans have determined magic does not exist, deciding instead to explain everything they can with science. When that fails, they turn to God. In today's age, very few can harness the magic around us even though they have the potential, and those who can, limit it to reading palms, balls, or cards. You did a good job of killing off the magic users throughout history—men and women.

"My kind, and a few other species, do know how to access that power, harnessing it to our own ends. If we take blood from someone stronger, our power will grow. For that reason, since I work within a high level of power, I am extremely careful who I let take my blood. It's a dangerous weapon to lend out."

"So...you *can* give each other blood, but it would give people unfair advantages. Like a car that can go a lot faster after a shot of NOS, but slows as the NOS runs out?"

"Yes."

"How long does it take to run out?"

"Depends on the power—or magic—level of the drinker, and that of the...donator."

"So, what about the other myths? Does your skin burn when the sun hits it?"

"No more than yours. Or maybe less—you are fairer than I. Irish decent?" He smiled at my furrowed brow. "As I said, we're nocturnal, mostly. We prefer the night. Our eyes are sensitive to light, for that reason. But some of my race has to blend in with humans. We have to do business and act like members of the community to maintain our assets. Protective lenses help that, but it's like one of your kind working a night job. It plays hell on the system."

I shook my head. "I'm not quite following."

"Humans have a chemical in their brains that reacts with light. Daylight means wake up. As night falls, their brain signals sleep time. That's a common issue with newborn babies—their brains are confused, thus having them waking and sleeping on—what humans deem—the incorrect schedule."

"And so...yours is backwards to ours, then?"

"You can be taught." His dark eyes sparkled. Seeing my glower, he changed the subject. "Were you taunting me earlier?"

"With the whole...secret room, thing?"

He nodded.

No sense beating around the bush. "Yes. Kind of."

His head quirked. "That's a dangerous game to play."

"I fought a giant with a whistle and a letter opener. I'm a slow learner."

"Yes, about that..." He shook his head and shifted in his seat. "How were you able to...fight Jonas off for so long?"

I shrugged. "I could...kinda...sense him coming; so I got out of the way."

He leaned forward, studying me, his gaze turning hard. "Your blade glowed red."

"Oh, thank God you saw it—I thought I was hallucinating!"

"But you're human..."

"Are you trying to convince me or yourself? Because I just want you to know I'm on board with those findings."

He shook his head. "Humans can't harness their power unless extensively trained. That's assuming we're able to find a human as open as you are. And yet..."

"I'm just as stumped as you are. Starting with that strange bull-headed creature talking to me. What were those? We haven't even—"

"What did you say?" the Boss stood in a rush, now towering over me. His eyes blazed, his face perfectly blank. "Did you say it *spoke* to you? Did you understand it?"

"Is that...*bad?*"

He was just about to take two steps toward me when the room froze over.

Speaking of strange...

Chapter Eleven

"Hey, bro, where you goin'?" Charles asked as Jonas burst through the door like his ass was on fire.

Jonas rounded on him, stabbing a finger back the way he'd come. "Fucking Boss has lost his mind! That stupid bitch-human attacked *me!* What the fuck was I supposed to do, let her continue to stab me?"

Charles reeled for a moment, trying to get his bearings. "The...bitch-human? You mean Sasha? She's *here?*"

Jonas stared at him. It looked like he was deciding if he should answer, or hurt Charles in some way. Charles kept talking to forestall a terrible decision.

"Well, what's she doing here? You didn't go get her, did you?"

"No I didn't go fucking get her! I don't know how the hell she found us, but she's got some tricks up her sleeve, I'll say that much. She can make her blade glow red—though her choice of blade is strange. Still, that's not normal for a human bitch. And her skin...she's not what she fucking seems—I'd bet she's working for the enemy, that's what I'd bet… Already been trained and trying to get in close to the Boss."

"She can…" Charles was having a hard time focusing within Jonas's hard stare. "But she's just a human."

"Exactly. She's just a fucking human. But yet, she's got magic. So now you tell me, is that fucking normal?"

Now Charles was having a hard time navigating the landmine of F-bombs, mostly because they were emphasizing Jonas's rage. Nothing good ever came from Jonas being in a rage. "Uh…"

"No! That is not fucking normal!" Jonas shouted into Charles's face. "But if fucking Boss thinks I am going to go slinkin' into the woods, hiding my face, then he's a fucking *fool!* I don't need this outfit! I got my own shit in the works!"

Confusion settled over Charles like a fog. "What's that suppo—"

Charles cut off as a prickling sensation tickled his scalp. "Can't be…"

Jonas swung his body toward the front of the house, disbelief masking his face. "Get the weapons!"

*****

The Boss burst into action, movements so fast I could barely make them out. He rushed to the far end of the room, touching and then swinging a lamp to open a hidden door in the wall's paneling.

Next, he dashed inside a closet, coming back with leather, swords, and knives. He bee-lined straight for me, all humor dried up. He was the man I'd always seen before tonight.

"Here," he said, thrusting a wicked looking dagger at me.

"What do I do with this?"

"Hopefully nothing. Otherwise, use it like that letter opener. Only this will work better."

As I gingerly held the shining hilt, curved like serpents at the end, the Boss shrugged out of his plain, long-sleeved tee-shirt, revealing his upper body. I stared, drool forming at the corners of my mouth. His body was perfection; toned and cut, meaty pecs and a chiseled six-pack. My brain shuddered to a stop as my body started to tingle. In addition to the tattoos on his arms, ancient runes cut down the side of his stomach, scrolling curled over his shoulder like smoke, or draped across a pec like a muscle accessory.

It was so. Damn. *Hawt*!

"You're distracting me," he said, shaking his head and taking a few steps back. He shrugged into a tight leather vest, then fastened his knives into holsters around his body. Next, he strapped on that wicked looking sword before shrugging on his large, leather duster.

"Why not a gun?" I asked, watching the ebb and flow of his body.

"Swords are cooler." He threw me a grin as he finished securing heavy boots, his hands blurring they moved so fast.

"But seriously…"

He straightened and grabbed my arm, narrowly missing my reflex to poke him in the arm with my knife.

"You're good with blades. What a surprising human you're turning out to be." He hustled me to the hidden doorway. "I'll explain about weapons at a later date. For now, make your way to the secret room."

He bent down and got right in my face, his commanding presence shocking into me when his beautiful dark eyes connected with mine. "Stay in that room, and stay safe! I will come for you when the danger has passed."

I barely felt the gentle shove into the dark corridor. The door banged shut, pitching me into total darkness. Still I stared and blinked, half confused how I could possibly be this turned on without bursting into flames. More, what the hell was this feeling that hated a separation from him, no matter how short, no matter how dire?

"I have absolutely lost my mind. There is no other explanation."

Taking a deep breath, my chest glowed warm, making the magic along the walls flash into color. I followed dumbly, my mind not in the present, still focusing on the non-man that tugged at my soul like he owned it.

When I stepped into the rectangle room, after nearly falling down two flights of stairs, I had no recollection of getting there. I was burning with lust, but freezing with that strange presence like I felt in the alleyway only a few nights ago. Or was it last night? I was losing time along with sanity.

I sat on the leather couch, watching the colors swirl around the room, wondering how many there were and how long this would take, when suddenly the air wrenched with a *bang*.

"What the—"

BOOM!

The walls shook.

What the hell is happening out there?

The colors in the room started to swirl madly, looking like the cartoon, *Alice in Wonderland,* on acid.

BOOM!

I paced, not liking to be caged up and safe, while a fight raged. Call me crazy—or just plain stupid—but I wanted to join the ranks and push back. That same feeling that always loved the thrill of high speed sung in me now, wanting action.

Then another thought struck me. Where was Jared? Why wasn't he in here?

In another flash of thought, I knew why. He was just a human, whereas I was a special kind of freak. In the land of insanity, where normal is mundane, Jared didn't rank nearly as high. Which meant, he was lying somewhere, hurt and afraid, completely forgotten about.

I was running before I knew which way I should go.

I burst out into chaos. Moving bodies were everywhere, clashing and fighting, flashes of light gleaming off colored blades, hacking and slashing. Women fought right alongside the men, faces aggressive, stabbing and slicing.

I had no idea which people represented my side. Or if I even *had* a side.

I weaved in and out of the large beings, hardly noticed, dodging and feinting with each butt pucker of warning. I allowed my sixth sense to lead, no idea where I was headed, just knowing that I needed to steer clear of the flying metal and somehow get to Jared.

Thank God these non-people didn't use guns—I wasn't lucky enough to effectively dodge stray bullets!

I sneaked through another room, having to weave through fewer numbers of fighting people—I could tell which warriors belonged to the house a little easier in this room on account of some were still naked—and let myself into a brightly lit space. Most of the house thus far had dimly lit, or hardly lit, rooms. This was the first with glaring bulbs and I found myself shielding my eyes for a minute while I adjusted.

Jared lay in a bed in the corner, huddled up and hugging his knees, clothed in a loose sheet. His eyes were wild and hair a mess. It looked like he was having the worst day of his life. And I was the reason for it.

Guilt would have to wait until tomorrow.

I darted after him as another colossal *BOOM* shook the foundation.

"C'mon Jared, let's get to safety!" I yelled over the noise.

BOOM!

"What's happening?" Jared asked in a small voice.

"Weird magic things, I think." I moved a shade and peered outside through the window.

Something with glowing purple eyes looked back.

"Oh crap!" I dropped the shade as if it was on fire. "Jared we've gotta go!"

"Home?"

"No—I don't know. Wait…maybe! Yes, home!"

Being that these people were predators worried about their territory, and I knew a thing or two about that since I was an avid fan of the Discovery Channel, I figured that this fight was the equivalent of one lion trying to kill the other lion and claim its mark. Only on a larger scale.

Even if I was wrong, this had nothing to do with me, and I didn't see any reason to hang out any longer than I had to.

I grabbed Jared and helped him to his feet. He gingerly waddled after me, and I didn't want to think why that was. He would need a blast of Forgetful Juice, but he'd need to be alive to get it, so first order of business was to get the hell outta here!

We made it halfway through the room when the window exploded. Glass sprayed the floor, nearly reaching us with its sharp and deadly blast. We turned slowly, mouths open, fear blossoming, as glowing purple eyes stared at me through the ragged shade hanging loosely in the jagged glass window.

"Oh shit!" I swore, feeling that *feeling* again. The one I felt before. Where my body started to flush, then heat, prickles sticking my arms, chest and head like acupuncture, awakening my senses. That substance in my middle blossomed, expanding, filling every inch of my body. My skin felt like it turned translucent, faster this time than the last, joy and ecstasy giving me a buoyancy unlike anything I have ever felt. I could have been flying, my feet soaring through the clouds. My laughter, pure and clean, bubbled up, drowning me. No man-made drug could possibly relate.

Purple eyes sparked. "I can promise you great rewards." The voice was disembodied, echoing in my mind, louder than thunder. Subtle. Curling into my ears with finesse. Stroking my brain and hugging that power blossoming in my chest.

My blade glowed red-orange, reminding me that these things were bad news. Whatever was zinging through my body like Prozac on steroids allured this thing, and I had a feeling my version of rewards were different than its own.

"Go. Now!" I yelled in the deadly quiet room.

Jared startled next to me, but continued to stare at the pulsing purple eyes.

"C'mon!" I ripped his arm with me, jerking his body to a start.

He staggered behind me as the foundation quaked beneath us, another blast sounding off to the far right. As we emerged into a dimly lit room, the walls started to glow again, not having been able to compete with the light from a moment before. The glow was weakened, though, as if whatever was happening outside was aimed at the very fiber of the house.

Clutching Jared's hand tightly, I contemplated which direction to go. Towards the front was the way I knew, but it was also bombarded. On my best day I might be able to sneak out, but no way could I get a lumbering Jared out behind me. The back was the next logical direction; but assuming there was a backyard, there had to be people loitering around. With swords.

So, Mr. Wizard, where did that leave us?

I took a deep breath, watching distractedly as a naked man shimmied his way across the room like a fencer, his long, pointed sword glowing blue-red as it whipped back and forth in front of an overwhelmed opponent. It wasn't the only thing whipping back and forth…

"Why is everyone always naked here?" Jared wheezed beside me.

"I've been wondering the same thing. C'mon, let's go."

Following my sixth sense, I walked quickly across the nearly empty room, turning a quick right, then another left, yanking Jared around, through and under fighting people waving swords. No one so much as glanced our way. I thought it very strange, but didn't want to stop and ask for a survey as to why.

We hit the room with the desk, the one where I'd watched the couple fornicating, and then halted. Being near the front of the house, this space was alive with activity. Swords and knives of all different colors tore through the air, landing ripping blows to opponents. Blood splattered the floor, people screamed and shouted, someone went flying past my line of sight and smashed into the wall like a floppy pile of limbs.

There was no way we could get to the secret door.

BOOOOM!!!

Jared and I fell back into the doorway, the ground quaking beneath our feet. The swirling colors in the walls swelled, like an electrical surge, before they dimmed. Then went out!

The hair rose on my arms. Something seriously wrong just went down, I could feel it. Whatever that color shifting was, it was meant for protection, and now it was gone.

The first monster entered the room.

It stood ten feet tall, like a Viking of old made out of rotten cheese, holding a flaming staff. It had no eyes, no nose, and for a mouth, a gaping hole filled with molten fire. As the first people from the house rushed it, the staff swept in a great arc, splitting two people in half as though they'd been made out of paper. The third person, holding a glowing red sword, a color to match the staff, blocked the sweep, causing a spray of red sparks from point of contact.

Another monster entered the room—it was the purple-eyed beast I saw earlier. And it was looking right at me!

"Run, Jared!" I hollered as that blossom in my chest rose, hearing a strange call in the air, and humming to join it.

I turned and pushed into Jared, like a kindergartner in a fire drill without a teacher to maintain order. I pushed him through the door, then dragged him behind me as I ran blindly, *knowing* those monsters entering the house were now looking for me. The word was out—whatever strange kind of thing I possessed, it was exactly the kind those monsters were looking for. Whether they were looking to extract or use, I had no idea, but I didn't get a rosy, sparkly slippers kind of feeling from the beasts.

I twisted and turned until I found another secret entrance. The only problem was, I was too rushed and freaked out to concentrate on how to open it! I closed my eyes and concentrated, a droplet of sweat working down my forehead.

"What are we doing?" Jared asked in hushed voice dripping with fear.

"*Shhhh!*" I put my fingertips to my temples, as if that would help. It didn't. I pinched the bridge of my nose, trying to *will* that sixth sense to be more obvious.

No luck.

I was in the beginning stages of kicking the wall when I felt it. My blood froze. My tongue got thick and my muscles sluggish. Jared had stopped breathing all together.

I turned in trepidation.

Chapter Twelve

Three human-shaped beings stood in the room with us, monsters all, each more horrible than the last. One had purplish horns covering the length of its body, blackened skin like a log after the fire has burned away. Another oozed some sort of liquid onto the floor—green, but pus-like; it emitted a putrid smell. The last was easily the worst. Its enormous head nearly touching the ceiling looked like it was made of writhing, angry worms, reddish in color, like maggots feasting on a bloody carcass.

It dawned on me that every monster I had seen had some sort of color attached to it. Each of those colors had existed in the swirling walls. These represented green, red, and purple. My knife was currently glowing a faint blue. That all meant something.

Since I didn't know what it meant, it didn't help me now.

"Jared, get behind me," I said in a shaking voice.

"What are you going to do?" Jared whispered, inching toward the wall.

"I haven't gotten that far, yet. I'm terrible at strategy."

My eyes darted throughout the room, looking for an exit, and finding three. The monsters blocked one. They were closer to another than we were, and we were backed against the third, unable to figure out its secret in order to use it. This was not looking good.

"Join us!" Puss Body said again, the horrible liquid creating a pool by its heinous clawed feet.

"I don't even want to touch you, let alone join you!"

A body emerged slowly from the side exit, hesitantly, trying to sneak. I kept my eyes on the monsters, hoping it was friend and not more foe. Jared touched the small of my back, sharing hope through touch.

Jonas appeared, blade in hand glowing dull orange. His eyes swept the room, lingering on the monsters. His hand tightened on his blade and his body bent slowly, ready to spring. As a stray thought, his gaze finished the sweep, finding me standing in front of Jared, tired and sweaty, dagger held in a meager arm. His eyes squinted. An evil smile curled his lips. He winked, and then backed slowly out of the room.

He was leaving us here to die.

Jared's hand started to shake.

The monsters advanced. They were coming to claim me, no doubt intending to kill Jared. He would get the better end of the bargain.

Knife in hand, tears in my eyes, I crouched. I would not go down without a fight. I'd get at least one or two holes in them before they got me!

It felt like electricity filled room, like a lightning bolt right before it touched down. My scalp tingled and my body broke out in shivers. The reddish maggot infestation monster was chanting.

"That is probably not good, Sasha," Jared warned, flattening himself against the wall.

He was right. A strange reddish smoke shivered in front of us, wafting in our direction.

What the hell did I do about smoke? How the hell did you poke holes in smoke?

I took a big breath, willing calm. My dagger flickered brighter, the color greenish now. Another breath. One more. The smoky circle came closer, within a few feet. The monsters advanced behind it, chanting something like a net into existence.

"Oh good, a net. That's not obvious or anything," I muttered, hand tightening, warmth in my chest now pulsing through my limbs.

The cloud wafted closer. I struck, slashing at it with my now -orangish knife. Where the blade passed, the smoke wilted like a flower, leaving the circle lopsided. I slashed again, and again, taking joy in the destruction of whatever the thing was, my hand moving faster than I would have ever thought possible, fueled by whatever warmth seeped from my chest.

"Sasha!" Jared pointed, his arm next to my face.

As the last of the smoky thing wilted and vanished, I looked up into the middle of the magical net, floating on its own.

Fear coursed through me. I didn't live through this much of my life to go down like this. And I certainly owed Jared a helluva lot more than what he'd been subjected to in the last few days.

Fear turned to anger. Anger boiled into determination. Determination dribbled into my chest, giving that warm blossom new life. Fresh blood. More power!

It surged and bubbled, filling me up and exploding over. My body was simmering, past joy, into an otherworldly plane. I reached farther, sucked in more. I pulled from the ground beneath me, from the walls surrounding me, from the charged air. I brought it in and lit it on fire.

As one of the monster's swords reached past me to Jared, and the net drifted around my body trying to capture me, I threw out my hands with one thing on my mind, *DIE!*

From my palms materialized blackness darker than night, more potent than acid. It flashed through the net and into the beings. Rather than bouncing off like light, it soaked into them, filling up the holes in their design—because someone else's design they were, like a constructed nightmare. The monsters exploded into wisps of air, like a dust bomb. Power shimmered in front of me, a nightmare vanishing with the dawn.

As the room cleared, my body wobbled, strength having left me with whatever I'd blasted from my palms. I fell to the ground in a limbless slide, already trying to shut off my brain from glowing knives, walking nightmares, and flashing palms.

"C'mon Sasha, we should go!" Jared whispered in a terrified voice, clutching my arm.

I staggered up, completely depleted. Everything was dark, objects in the room hard to see. We ambled along, Jared basically leading, until we got to a door standing wide open, screams drifting through like fog on the ocean.

"This is the way they brought me in. There is a parking lot beyond here," Jared hissed, plucking at my arm.

"That is very useful information, Jared. I only wish you'd said something earlier."

I lurched through the door, hitting the door jam and careening off, landing on my face in the dirt. Jared hoisted me back up, practically dragging me along, until we got to a car. I had no idea how he opened the door, but I do know he shoved me in right before I saw black.

*****

A blood curdling scream pierced the fight right before every *Dulcha* in sight exploded, bursting outward like dirt clods, and then vanishing. The air electrified, as if great power had been unleashed in a wild, raw upsurge.

Warriors looked around, unsure of what just happened or what might've caused it. Enemies stared at each other across their swords. Suddenly, they realized the scales had tipped. No longer was the aggressing party winning. It was universally known and seldom disputed that the Boss and his men could not be beaten when it came down strictly to sword work.

That is what had the Eastern Territory running—fleeing down the street and out of sight.

"What the hell caused that, Boss?" Charles asked with panting breath and bleeding arms, stepping up beside him as they watched grown males sprinting to their cars or down the street.

Stefan shook his head. "I would've said their mage, but it was his creations that were destroyed." He shook his head again, putting his hands on his hips and surveying the landscape. Small fires lit the grass and small shrubs. Bodies lay strewn in ragged clumps, skin slick with blood. This had been a grizzly battle with a lot of power—Stefan was afraid to count their losses. He lost good men tonight, not to mention friends.

"They're getting bold, now." Stefan looked back out to the street where his best spell casters were trying to do damage control. This neighborhood was more oblivious than most, thanks to their constant spell working, but the magnitude of the fight would draw some notice, even with their thick charms. "We haven't had an attack directly to our castle in...I don't even remember a time."

"Boss!" Jameson sprinted up, winded and bloody. But alive. "The human police are on their way. I'm trying to clear the house, but it might be best if we get Luke."

Luke was the best they had with pheromones. He was subtle but effective, easily able to navigate even the most difficult human. Stefan wanted to pit him against Sasha and see if the male had some effect.

"Go to it," Stefan said with a nod, thoughts sticking to the pesky human that seemed to follow him like a bad smell. *Good* smell, actually—it turned him on something fierce. It didn't change the fact that she seemed to turn up wherever he was, staring at him, bringing others toward his hiding places, and needing constant pushing to make sure she stayed gone. Only to find out she wasn't gone at all. It was almost laughable. And would have been, if it had been somebody else's problem.

He longed to be rid of her. She had a strange effect on him; he was aware of her, always. If she was anywhere close, he could identify her whereabouts without thought. It were as if a cable connected them. He had no idea how to get rid of it, and now that they knew she could withstand their influence, and also had magic, things would only get more complicated.

He needed to figure out who he could pawn her off on.

He entered the house and groaned. The furniture was mostly in tatters, the walls coated with burn marks, and bodies littered the floor.

"How many have we lost?" Stefan asked Charles, trying not to let his head slip downward or his voice waver. He couldn't allow the others to see his weakness. He would mourn the losses on his own time.

Charles shook his head in small movements. "They're being rounded up. What should we do with the enemy?"

"Put 'em on a tarp in the front. If the E.T. want to come back for them, so be it. We will not stoop to their caliber of disgusting."

"Yes, Boss."

"Fetch the humans. I want to get them out of my hair."

"Yes, Boss."

Stefan bent to a body, realized it wasn't one of his, and then froze. Not ten minutes ago he'd reflected that he knew when that blasted human was near. At the moment, she wasn't. Which meant, she took off.

With the enemy.

The building shook with his anger, swirls of power called up in his rage. He did not tolerate spies.

Chapter Thirteen

"Sasha? Are you okay? Sasha?"

I opened my bleary eyes to Jared's worried face. I raised my head a fraction, then immediately lowered it again, my cheek resting against my soft down comforter. The squashy material didn't help my pounding headache. I moaned.

"Sasha?"

"I'm alive, Jared, please stop yelling in my ear."

"Okay, but do we need to go to the hospital? You don't look good."

Knowing that Jared was prone to over-reacting, I closed my eyes again. "Aspirin."

"Yup, sure, you got it!"

I sat up slowly, my head swimming in dizzy circles, to receive a glass of water and two white pills. After swallowing those down, I steadied myself against the nightstand. I felt like I had a fever. My skin was oversensitive, my forehead slick with sweat, and my body shivering with cold. Every muscle ached to the bone, my hands shook, and my head pounded. I also might...

I barely made it to the toilet.

Hanging with my head half a foot from my dinner, I sprawled out, still shivering, waiting for the next wave of...

"Do you want me to hold your hair?"

I waved Jared away as I dry heaved. After I finished, another feeling washed over me.

"Get out, quick!" I screamed, needing to swap ends.

As Jared sprinted from the bathroom, not arguing with the next wave of bodily fluid to pay homage to the porcelain god, I started a marathon of moaning. I felt like I was dying.

And if I wasn't dying, I wanted to.

"Sasha, we gotta get outta here!" Jared screamed through the door.

"I can't go far without creating a very messy trail of bread crumbs..."

"He's here! That big one! He's *here!*"

Fear pierced my gut. It wasn't the only thing. I definitely wasn't moving. "Who? Which guy?"

"The one they are all scared of!"

I pushed the wind out of my lungs in a huge sigh of relief. The Boss. Then I moaned, leaning against the wall in utter misery. Even if it had been Jonas, I wouldn't be able to do much. I wouldn't even be able to move off the toilet.

A horrible *bang* permeated the door to the bathroom, a follow-up chorus of wood splintering. Male shouting competed with my moans of agony. My vision wavered and my thoughts muddled. I was getting worse.

The door next to me burst open, the hinges cracking and frame splintering. I barely heard the thud even though I was three feet away, shivering on the toilet. The Boss stood over me, some sort of accusation on his lips, before his eyebrows dipped low over his eyes.

"While this situation probably couldn't get much worse, you are certainly making it ten times more awkward," I slurred, barely able to keep my eyes open. My arms hung loose at my sides, dragging my shoulders down like weights.

"What's happened?" He bent to me, opening my right eye with his big thumb and finger.

"Careful," I warned, trying to pull my head away.

I felt my head clutched in his mighty paw before I, once again, lost consciousness.

"C'mon Sasha, take a sip. Just a sip, Sasha, c'mon."

My head lolled across a large shoulder. I couldn't feel my body. It was light outside, the sun's rays filtered through heavy curtains, sprinkling my face.

"C'mon now, sweetie, drink a little."

What felt like skin pressed against my lips, a warm liquid dripping into my mouth. I tried to move away from the salty, metallic taste, but I had no strength. More of the substance oozed between my lips, my throat involuntarily gulping it down to clear it from choking me.

More dribbled into my mouth, filling it up, before I swallowed again. And again. Warmth started to spread throughout my chest, making my limbs tingle.

"That's enough," a man's voice said to my right. "She is unused to this. We don't want her body to reject it. She'll surely die, then."

I knew a moment of panic before sleep gobbled me up.

Chapter Fourteen

Stefan sat down at his desk, tired and strung out. He should get some sleep; it'd been over twenty-four hours since he last lay down. But there was work to be done.

He rubbed his eyes and stared down at Jameson's report. They'd lost over a dozen men and women—decent fighters, but not the best. It was nowhere near as bad as he'd thought. As far as his people could tell, most of the injuries had come from blades in the hands of mortals, not the *Dulcha*. It was as if magical creations had lost interest in the battle half-way through.

Stefan shook his head and leaned back. He needed to call a council. They needed to train someone to fill Stefan's clan's mage role. The E.T. were the biggest upstarts wanting to expose themselves to humans in a great many years. Stefan was fighting lopsided without a strong magic thrower to compete. All Trek, their White mage, did now was hone his craft, readying his crew to take out Stefan and reach out their hand. This turf war would become a national war quickly, with everyone seeking grandeur stepping up by Trek's side. It would be damned hard to stop him, especially since the Council, which should've already stepped in, were a bunch of old fools waiting around and hoping for a peaceful resolution to fall out of their asses.

"Boss?"

Charles stood in the doorway with a plate of food.

"Yes, Charles, come in."

The young male approached the large desk and laid the tray of stew to the side. He took a seat in one of the visitor chairs facing Stefan. "You wanted to see me, sir?"

Stefan willed himself wakefulness as he beheld the eager warrior. "Yes, Charles. I'm assigning you to the human. I want her watched at all times. She very nearly died from excessive magic usage, which means she has it in large enough supply to pose a threat. We will want to test her, see if we can train her; use her. Until then, however, we'll need to make sure she doesn't harm herself or anyone else."

Charles looked like he'd just swallowed a slug. "And the boyfriend?"

"Will lose his memory and never be touched again; is that clear?"

"Absolutely! Yup, yes it is. I didn't even want to in the first place—guys aren't really my thing. I mean, yes, they'll do in a pinch, but if I had—"

Charles stopped babbling as Stefan hardened his stare. The other male's eyes found the floor in a hurry.

"You will need to change your schedule to match hers. I want to be updated on all large goings-on. I want her kept away from here, by force if necessary, and I do not want weapons at her disposal."

Charles bobbed his head in acknowledgement.

Stefan matched the nod with one of his own. Then sighed. "It is a damned irritating distraction at a time like this."

"Can I take a shot at her?" Charles asked sheepishly. "I've wanted to since I saw her."

A sudden flash of rage burst through Stefan's insides. He had to stop himself from clenching his fists. "It seems we can't beguile her, though I plan to test that theory, and she's hung up on this boyfriend of hers. I doubt she'll have you. But…" He let his breath out in a controlled exhale. "You're welcome to try, so long as you don't push her boundaries in any way."

"Yes, sir."

The male sounded gleeful. And yes, the human had something that seemed to call, seemed to tug a male's vitals until he could barely think, but she wasn't worth the hassle. Not to mention she had yet to really explore her sexual side, and was probably entirely boring in the sack.

So why the hell was the thought of her with another man pinching his insides and making him want to rip someone's arms off?

Charles interrupted Stefan's thoughts by saying, "Have you chosen a mate yet, sir?"

And then there was that little problem. "No."

"Excuse me for saying, but you have the pick of the breed-able females—anyone you want can be yours…"

Stefan rubbed his eyes. There were some exquisite beauties with high levels of power, all right; each ready to throw herself at him. Based on his position and his own high level of power, he needed to bond with someone and create offspring—or try, anyway. He just…didn't want to bother. He didn't want a female to have a claim on him. They were all too concerned with his position, or his time, or his conversation. Plus, he hated sharing his bed. He could never sleep when someone was breathing on him.

He waved the thought away. "I don't have to make the decision for a few more months."

"Eenie, meenie, miney, huh?" Charles grinned. Then dropped his eyes again when he felt the heat of the stare.

"You're excused," Stefan said in clipped tones.

Stefan was just about to get up and finally head to bed when Charles stepped aside from the door and turned his body. Thinking the young man wanted to discuss something further, Stefan waited, then wished he hadn't. A slinky woman in four inch heels and a see-through chemise wandered in, all hip and breast.

Speaking of possible mates.

"Hi, baby," she said in a lioness purr.

Charles hovered in the door, wondering if he'd be invited to play. Which would just take longer. Stefan minutely shook his head.

"Hello, Darla. What brings you?"

She wound her way to his side of the desk, her nipples puckered in arousal. She heaved herself onto the desk in front of him, legs draping to each side of his chair, her bare sex spreading for his inspection.

He felt a stirring in his groin as she said, "I just wanted to drop in and say hi. See how you were…" She gracefully pushed herself forward until she sat high on his lap, pushing down on his hardening manhood. Her body leaned back, putting her perfect breasts on display through her sheer top.

He was dead tired, melancholy from the men and women he lost, distracted from the irritating human and her magic issues, and really just wanted to head up to bed. But now he had an erection.

First thing's first.

He ran his hands up her thighs, pushing the fabric up with it. Up her stomach and over her chest, he slipped the fabric over her head and into a bunch on the desk. He bent forward, taking a taut nipple in his mouth and sucking, lightly sticking it with his teeth. A small amount of blood trickled out over his tongue, tasting of sweet cherries.

"Hmmmm," she moaned, rubbing her crotch against his in graceful hip swings, experienced and practiced at the best way to get a man off.

Suddenly he needed a good, hard screw.

He grabbed her hips and lifted her body off of him, placing her butt onto the desk. She leaned back like a stretching cat, her feet out to the sides, exposing that lovely pink center. As he ripped down his zipper, he ran his tongue up her slit, tasting salt and sex. She'd been active earlier, he could taste it on her, which wouldn't be unusual if it wasn't for the battle.

Taking himself out, he kissed and licked up her body, once again focusing on a perfect breast while he stroked himself up, getting hard enough to get this underway. At the right level of turned on—which, these days, was usually just *good enough*—he laid his body over hers and pushed the head of his dick just past her outer lips. With one big push, he pumped himself all the way in, his hips hitting against her ends. Not wasting any time, he slammed into her, deep and hard, taking out his frustration on the world with her sweet sex.

"Yes, Boss. Harder! Yes!" she moaned, clutching her hair in fistfuls as her breasts bounced up and back with his rhythm.

Stefan put his body low over her, swiveling his hips, his cock working up a nice, wet friction against her inner walls. He worked harder, thinking of the human's smell trapped in his secret den—a place which she shouldn't have found on her own. It was spicy and fragrant, trapping his senses.

"Oh you're so *hard!*" Darla moaned, pumping her sex up to meet his thrusts.

Stefan's balls were starting to constrict, the room ringing with wet slapping as his body hammered off of hers. Sweating and panting, Darla reached forward, her eyes closed, her face one of bliss, and clutched onto him, scraping those sexy nipples off of his chest.

Stefan's eyes rolled up in the back of his head as his cock erupted, filling her. Three more thrusts and he was emptied.

"Hmmm, that was nice," Darla said, leaning back on the desk, her hand trailing down between her breasts.

Out of breath, Stefan straightened up and fastened his pants. He nodded. "I'll see you."

"Soon." She laughed in a low, throaty voice as he made his way out of the room. She was under the impression she all but had the mate title.

And realistically, she was probably right.

*****

I blinked my eyes in the bright sunlight. I was positioned directly under a window with the shade up, in direct line with the sun. I blocked the glare with my palm, squinting around the room. One glance told me where I was, and the second told me who I was with. I rolled so my head was on the pillow and groaned.

"Good mid-morning," Charles said in a tired, gruff voice.

He sat off to the side in a large, vintage chair with velvet arms. He held knitting equipment that he quickly let fall to his lap in anticipation of conversation. Which apparently meant we had to have one.

"Hi." My voice was just as gruff and tired. "I feel like a drowned rat."

"That's because you *look* like a drowned rat."

I grunted, rolling to the very edge of the bed so the sun wasn't beating down on me. I sat up slowly, clutching my head to keep it from exploding. "What happened after I passed out?"

"A few things, mostly concerning bodily fluid. All over my car."

A humiliated glance told me he wasn't upset somehow. I mumbled out an extremely embarrassed, "Sorry…"

"Eh," he shrugged. "Once I threw up all over Jonas when I had too much to drink. Then I got my ass beat. It happens."

I didn't know what to say to that.

"So anyway…feeling horny? I know I am…"

I couldn't help but wheeze out a laugh. It was hard to take the guy seriously. "No, I'm not really in the mood."

He shrugged, unconcerned. "I figured, what with the near death incident, but it never hurts to ask."

"I nearly died? What do you mean?"

"Too big of a magical release. Who would've thought a human would have enough magic for that, huh? Go figure. But there you go."

My head wrapped around the information slowly, the term unfamiliar anywhere but with a clown and a wand. "Magic? Me?"

My memory drifted back to that black stuff that shot out of my palms. It had felt like my insides were pulled out through my fingertips until I had nothing left to fill my body. Shortly thereafter I'd felt like I had the worst fever imaginable.

It made a lot more sense than I wanted it to. So I switched gears immediately. "Where's Jared?"

"His mind was wiped and his body deposited back with his orange headed roommate. They're both being kept in their rooms until all our influence wears off. Jared's going to be a little spacey for a while, though—we had a lot of emotional damage to try and hide."

"How do you do it? Erase memories?"

"Oh, we don't exactly *erase* them. They're still there, we just, kinda, cover it up. Hide it. Like really old memories that you thought were gone. Dreams will bring them back up, but everyone assumes dreams are just imaginary, so..."

My head felt like it was stuffed with cotton. I nodded, unable to process any more. "When can I go home? I have a class later this afternoon."

He laughed, picking up his knitting. "You couldn't even walk out of here if you tried, but you want to go to school? Tenacious. And dumb. No, Mira is taking care of that. She'll go in your place until you're well enough. She's pretty smart! She has her doctorate in physics, I think. A little glamour in the right places, and actually doing your homework—something you apparently fail to do half the time..." he tsk'ed at me, "and *voila,* great grade."

"But..."

"Plus, we're still not 100% sure you're accepting the Boss's blood. You seem like you're recovering, but sometimes humans' bodies reject the potency of the magic. Usually, the first few times, you'd get blood from someone with a lower level of power to see your reaction, but you were too far gone."

"The Boss's blood?" My voice sounded hollow. I vaguely remembered choking down metallic tasting liquid, but I'd had no idea what it was. Or *whose* it was.

"Yes. Shocking, right? I know. He hasn't given his blood to anyone since he became the leader of this territory. But he's the strongest, most powerful of us, and if anyone could've saved you, it was him. His idea, too. Good guy, that Boss. We're in good hands with him, even though we're against a pretty powerful mage."

Half of me found all this fascinating. This was another life, one I hadn't known even existed outside of my weird hallucinations, a few short days ago. The other half of me just wanted him to stop talking. Even though he seemed sweet, he was uncommonly chatty, and with the state of my body and head at the moment, I just wanted quiet.

To that end, I lay back down, then immediately tried to fight off an overanxious sun. Eyes squeezed shut, I turned my face at Charles. "Can I ask you to lower the shade, please? The sun is blinding me."

"And here I thought humans worshipped the sun." He shook his head, his large body crossing the room to wrangle the shade. "Makes me tired, that's all I know."

"What's with the knitting?" I asked sleepily, shifting to the center of the pillow. It felt like my veins were filled with lead. It hurt just to be awake.

As Charles sat back down, he said, "What do you mean?"

"Only old women knit."

"Well, now, that's just rude. And not true. I have made many a fine scarf, which I will prove by knitting *you* a fine scarf."

I shook my head, a smile working onto my face. I meant to ask if he was guarding me, or comforting me until I felt better, but sleep pulled me under before I could harvest another thought.

Chapter Fifteen

"Ready?" Charles asked, holding open the door.

I'd spent two days on bed rest, letting my "natural resources" regenerate within the confines of my designated room within the mansion. That's all Charles would tell me about my situation, "You were depleted, and you need to regenerate your natural resources. The Boss is powerful, but he isn't a pack of gods." Peppering him for information yielded no results, but plenty of requests for sex. Worse, I wasn't even allowed to wander the halls or have a peek outside; I was on lockdown, Charles being my chatty and jolly jailer.

When the order came down the line that I could go, which was ten minutes ago, I didn't need to be told twice. I was tired of the constant surveillance, I wasn't a huge fan of the scarf in progress—red and orange wouldn't go with anything in my closet—and I needed some freedom. I needed my life back! This new world was interesting, and the prospect of having magic fascinated me, but I could only handle so many changes at one time. I needed a little time to get used to all this.

"Ready, Freddy!" I snatched up my car keys.

"Who's Freddy?" Charles asked in confusion, guiding my arm toward the right.

"Your momma."

"Is this some weird human joke?"

"Yes, and you are the butt of it."

"Well, you are just a butt. Head!"

"Terrible joke."

"You suck," he pouted.

"Now you're just being mean."

We strolled at a measured pace through empty halls and rooms, the damage from a few nights ago greatly on the mend, the replaced furnishings a little more modern, but with the same quality.

"Do you guys work? How do you afford all this?" I asked, scanning the art on the walls with interest. They were largely oil paintings, huge, and appeared expensive, though I was no art dealer. "And where is everyone?"

"We are often left a portion of people's estates—usually a new friend that happened to grow a firm attachment right before they died. We then have excellent investors and business personnel within our fold."

"Your fold?"

"Yeah, you know, our bros. Anyway, if we don't make it ourselves, kind humans are nice enough to donate it to us, and then we take great care of it. The Boss is excellent at management."

"Ah. And the half-naked people having loud, obnoxious sex that occasionally woke me up over the last couple days?"

"Probably fully naked, and they are most likely sleeping. It's late. Or early, depending on your take."

"Oh yeah, I forgot you guys keep the opposite schedule."

"Better get used to it, because once you start testing for magic, you'll have to change your sleeping schedule around. Thankfully! I'm not used to this. We need to get you in trouble soon so I have something to do."

As we emerged from the house, I stopped, preventing him from stepping outside with me. "What do you mean?"

"Didn't the Boss tell you? You'll have to be tested for magic. We'll bring you back here for that; but we can't keep an assessing team up for you…"

"No, I mean, why would my getting in trouble give you something to do?"

Charles tilted his striking face, one shapely eyebrow quirking quizzically. "I'm confused."

"Because he'll be keeping an eye on you," said another voice.

It felt like my stomach was on a rollercoaster, launching high into the air, and then plummeting a second later. I turned to the right slowly, my body tingling.

The Boss stood next to me, having snuck up without a sound. He wore a vest, his bare arms cut and defined, circled by those swirling, and sometimes vicious looking, tattoos. His perfect face was turned down to me, his eyes squinting in the noon sun, but the velvety black within sucking me in and turning my chest to goo.

I unconsciously stepped forward, my body too weak to resist the pull. The invisible string attaching our bodies tugged, warming my limbs.

A female throat cleared as my eyes held his. Only then did I realize someone stood next to him. A distractingly beautiful woman, over six feet tall, glared down at me, her dark brown eyes hard. It was then I noticed the red high heels, the same ones I noticed when I was under the desk a few days ago and she was with someone that was not the Boss.

The way she was standing, though, pushed in close to the Boss's side, her chest angled toward him, immediately registered as having a claim on him. Or wanting one. Being that the Boss allowed the body proximity, I got the impression the feeling was mutual.

A surge of jealousy reared its head as I took a shuffling step backward, backing down from her territorial stare.

"Aren't you going to introduce us, Boss?" Her voice was melodic—if playing a xylophone made of icicles could be called musical.

The Boss, apparently having a real name, glanced at her before focusing on me again. "No, she is unimportant." To me, he said, "Charles will be watching you. Our memory charms don't seem to stick, which means you're a liability to our lifestyle. I cannot risk a loose mouth. Should you decide to mention us to anyone—including your boyfriend—I will kill you *and* the receiver of information. Do I make myself clear?"

"Wow, when did you become such a jerk?" I muttered, stuffing my hands in my pockets.

"An occasional side effect of power," Charles commented absently. He quickly lowered his eyes and hunched within Stefan's hard stare, trying to turn invisible.

Black eyes flashed back to me. "I will contact you in a few weeks for testing. Stay out of trouble."

He walked into the house, his back straight and muscled, the memory of his handsome face etched into my consciousness, quickly ruined by the slinky body and condescending stare of his lady love as she followed him inside.

"What's *her* problem?" I muttered in a sulky tone.

"First off, she's a bitch." Charles stepped outside and immediately fastened some sunglasses on my face.

"I don't need—"

"Shush, the sun is hard on the ol' peepers. C'mon." Charles gave me a shove in the direction of my car across the street, a few new scratches worked down the side of the fading red paint. He put his own sunglasses on, following me, before saying, "Second, she is probably going to be mated to that unlucky bastard—don't tell him I called him a bastard—and is most likely pissed that he gave some dumb human blood but won't pony up to her. No offense. You're not dumb, but she probably doesn't care. Anyway, she is an ambitious little soldier—she tries to use her beauty and great knack-in-the-sack to suck as much blood as possible to improve from red level to orange. People are on to her, but she can be…persuasive. I steer clear.

"Unfortunately for the Boss, she is prime real estate for a baby maker. She's had one miscarriage already, her mother had two kids, and her grandmother had three. Good blood line. And you know, there's the beauty, and the swirly hip thing she does, and her father is high in politics—she's the best choice in a textbook sort of way. Although, you don't seem to read your textbooks, so I guess you wouldn't subscribe to the same views."

"She miscarried his baby? That's a good thing? Also…what the hell does baby making have to do with marriage? Don't you people like each other?"

Charles laughed as he folded into my car. "It probably wasn't his that she miscarried; but yes, it's good. It means she is fertile. He is powerful and our leader, he needs offspring. He also needs stability and a co-leader. She can provide all that. Just sucks she's a bitch, know what I mean? Hot, though."

"So…you guys have sex all the time, not protected, and get excited when you randomly get pregnant, father unknown?"

"Humans wouldn't understand—you guys breed like rabbits. You so much as look at each other with heat and you get pregnant."

"So, you're probably super sexual because of a need to reproduce?" I guessed.

"No, Dr. Over-Analyze-Everything, it feels good. But we don't protect ourselves hoping we can work up a little procreation. Otherwise, we are just a dying breed of amaze-balls."

"Seriously, how old are you?" I mumbled, turning into my parking spot. "And more importantly, where do you plan to sleep?"

"In human years, probably about sixteen. In our years, I'm thirty-eight. And in your bed. With you. Naked." He waggled his eyebrows, probably trying for some sort of suggestive turn-on.

It had the opposite effect. "You aren't sleeping with me, and do you use human years like we use dog years?"

"If the shoe fits."

I shook my head. There was no point trying to figure out the fork in the evolutionary road all in one sitting. Especially with the equivalent of a teenage boy. I cut our dialogue off by calling him a douche.

As I got out of the car, I restarted the conversation with, "Why was Stefan such a dick to me?"

"Eh," Charles waved the comment away with his hand. "He's just trying to be all big-time and all that. He's cool on a personal level, but a little stressed out and bitchy when he's got a lot of people following him around. Plus, I don't think he knows what the hell to do with you. You're a complete anomaly, and he doesn't like unexplained crap. Freaks him out. Although, admitting that would basically be saying he's a weak Nancy-boy, which would then make him have to kill somebody to set the record straight, so…yeah, he can be a dick."

"You need to work on summarizing."

"You need to work on opening your legs. Crap, I forgot how small this apartment is."

I woke up slowly, something eating away at my conscious mind, dragging my thoughts out of the dream world. Someone panted, as though in pleasure. A small sound, like a continual slide of hand on soft velvet, drifted to me from the floor.

"Charles?"

The sound stopped. "Yeah?" The sound started up again.

I sprang to a seated position, spying Charles lying on his blow-up mattress with the sheets around his ankles, his fist pumping his large erection.

"What the hell are you doing?" I screeched.

He stopped again, hand halfway down his shaft. He blinked up at me, his well-built chest halfway lifted off the mattress. "What do you mean?"

"Are you *masturbating?*"

He shook his head with a dramatic eye blink, ending with wide, disbelief filled eyes. "I'm certainly not trying to rip my cock off. What else would I be doing with it?"

"Well cut it out! I'm in the same room, for God sakes. What's wrong with you?"

"For one, I have to do this myself. What has my life come to that I can't get someone to play with my bells and whistle? Wait, speaking of whistle, didn't you say you had one? 'Cause I bet this blows the same as that. Care to try it out?"

I couldn't stop a crooked smile from working up my face. "Just…cut it out, okay? I don't need you jacking off in here."

"It turns you on…"

"*Everything* turns me on lately. I have no idea why, but only animals succumb to it."

"Animals obviously have more fun. Seriously, I can prove it—"

"Gross!"

"No! You took that wrong. I meant, like, I was wild 'n shit. Not that I'd *done* it with an animal. Gross. Although—"

"Stop right there!"

"No! I was just—" Charles cut off, his expression melting from humor to slightly concerned.

That was when I felt the chill descend, settling firmly into my bones. "Please, no. Not again!"

Charles was up in a second, braced in front of me with an erection and a glowing orange blade. I didn't even have time to wonder where the weapon came from before my door burst inward, catching me with a corner and hurling me off the bed.

I popped up from behind the mattress, my hand antsy to grab a weapon. Instead, I only had that Goddamn whistle! I snatched it anyway as a glowing blue blob filled the doorway.

"They didn't send the heavy artillery, but why did they send anything at all?" Charles mused, his blade whirling so fast all I noticed were streaks of orange cutting through the dark room.

"Is it just the one?" I asked with an even voice.

Why the hell wasn't I scared? I'd almost been captured by a couple of these things not that long ago.

"Charles, are you scared?"

Charles leapt forward, his sword slicing through a projectile object separating from the blob body in the rough shape of a claw. The severed tentacle poofed into blue vapor, wafting through the air before disappearing.

"Don't ask..." He lunged again, his blade whirling, slicing a chunk out of the entity before it could form another claw. "...stupid questions."

A third slice had the thing cut in half, the pieces not able to slide apart before two more slashes carved it out of existence.

Charles stepped back, wiping his forehead with his forearm.

I stared at his glistening body, droplets of sweat working down his corded muscle, identifying each grove with precision. My mind slipped to the Boss without my control.

I registered a phone ringing as Charles slowly turned to me, his manhood starting to rise again. His eyes burned into me as his head tilted to the side. "For a prude, you are sure turned on a lot."

That snapped me out of it. I deflected immediately. "You're freaking naked while fighting monsters and swinging a sword. You have all that bare *muscle!"* I stabbed a finger at him in accusation. "How is that my fault?"

A smile wormed up his face. I registered my phone ringing again.

"Aren't you going to answer it? Or are you ready to give me a go?" Charles's expression was gleeful.

"Oh, shut up." I snatched my phone out of my handbag, registering the name as Jared.

A jolt of fear pierced my gut. I gouged the phone as I raised it up to my ear. "Jared?"

"Sasha, help! Something is trying to get in!"

Charles stood right in front of me, bent at the waist, his ear angled to my head. After hearing Jared, his body straightened with a jerk. His eyes bored into mine, the shadows sprinkling across his face, one smoky gray eye standing out.

"I have to go." I threw the phone back into my bag.

Charles shook his head slowly. "You have magic. He doesn't. I can't let you."

"They'll kill him!" Heat engulfed my body, my awareness now recognizing that as magic. My limbs tingled, my chest felt like it flexed, then opened, the magic coating my skin and branching out, at my beck and call.

"Sorry, Sasha, I can't let you go."

His hand grabbed my arm so fast I didn't see it coming. Which didn't change the result. As his fingers clasped my skin, the tiny sound of skin searing had him flinching away a second later.

"What the—"

I was running before he'd finished the sentence.

Bare feet slapping on pavement, my handbag flapping at my side, I flew to my car in desperation, knowing that Charles would be right behind me. Sure enough, just as my door closed, his giant fist smashed through the window.

"Same side!" I screamed, fragments of shatterproof glass raining in on me.

I slammed the car in reverse and stomped on the pedal. The car lurched backward, Charles falling, naked, onto the empty parking space. I flung the gear into drive and punched the pedal again, taking off as Charles started sprinting after me.

Another thrill of fear slammed into me, only this time, it energized me. My smile took up my whole face as Charles chased me, butt-ass naked, sprinting with bare feet on concrete, muscles rippling, a phone to his ear.

He grabbed a phone but no shoes? What was the story with his priorities?

He was quick, but he couldn't match the speed of my Firebird. Especially when I'd been given a green light to go fast. Recklessly fast.

Chapter Sixteen

I screeched to a halt in front of Jared's apartment complex. It took me three seconds to register that unnatural cold. One or more of those beasts were here, and judging by the freezing marrow in my bones, it was probably leaning towards *more.*

I sprinted up the walkway and through the door balancing precariously on one hinge. The light in the entryway of the apartment complex flickered, a telltale sign that something was horrifically amiss. At least, that was always the case in horror movies. Then again, the rent here was cheap, and the landlord never got around to fixing anything. It might have been normal.

Still, the door was broken. Something was amiss.

I sprinted up the stairs, my sanity having been left in my apartment. On Jared's floor I heard screaming. Loud, high-pitched, unnatural screaming, like a rabbit that felt the first pinch of the wolf's jaws.

A burst of speed had me standing in the doorway of Jared's apartment, staring at two…*things*. One looked like a four legged spider, equipped with red mandibles and grisly brown fur. Maybe human once, maybe all creation, this thing was so unnatural my stomach started to twist. Beside it stood an alien—oval head, long limbs and bulbous kind of fingers.

I blinked a few times, not believing my eyes. Somehow, the weird spider thing made sense. I'd seen some pretty gross monsters lately. The alien-looking thing, though, seemed a bit…childish somehow. Like the conjurer was telling some sort of joke.

Or it really was an alien…

Clearing my mind of the panicked fog, I zeroed in on what could only be the remnants of a human. Red head lulled, eyes staring, face slack. His body bent unnaturally, his heels able to touch his head, like his back had been broken.

I stared, horror creeping into my awareness eradicating every other feeling. Rubber limbs fell to the floor, the body splayed unnaturally, dead.

At the back of the apartment another scream erupted. My gaze drifted that direction, my body numb. A giant held Jared by the hair, my boyfriend crying and screaming, scratching at the hand carrying him by his scalp.

This wasn't a monster.

Hazel eyes flashed to mine, connecting us in a moment. Power pulsed inside of me, registering the danger. My forehead beaded with sweat. That's when the monsters turned toward me slowly. They honed in on me, sensing the magic I knew called to them like a turkey leg to a starving man.

The man's eyebrows dipped in confusion, his head tilted. He slowed.

"What is this?" A voice of masculine honey poured across the apartment floor, crawling up my legs and covering me with slime.

Something wasn't right with this man, besides the fact that he carried my boyfriend by his hair.

"Come to rescue your love? I heard him calling someone—you? Why not the police, I wonder. And why…" The monsters stepped toward me. My chest throbbed. The man's eyes turned calculating. "Bring her with us."

Power pulsed through the room—from me or them, I had no idea. Sweat dribbled down my forehead. The man kept coming, Jared screaming and crying in his grip.

I tried to push them back, like I'd done before. I stuck out my palms, desperately trying to destroy them somehow, but I didn't know what had caused it. Maybe fear deterred me. Maybe my near-death experience had me holding back. Whatever it was, nothing came!

"Shit." I grabbed a baseball bat, ready to go down fighting.

It didn't glow. Maybe that was reserved for metal?

No matter. I played softball once.

As the first creature reached me, I swung with all my might. Then staggered sideways and forward, the bat going clean through the creation.

A cartoon-like hand reached for me, fire erupting on my shoulder where it touched. Blisters formed, the pain consuming me, when suddenly I was flying.

I fell to the left, barreling into a cheap bookcase that splintered under my weight. A leather clad man stood in my wake, burnished gold sword flashing, bare arms swirling with the same burnished gold light, his tattoos glowing and crawling around his skin.

I felt a strange stirring in my core, like I lay in the middle of a feather storm. Burnished gold materialized around me, forming a cage. A churning, vibrating cage, keeping me imprisoned.

What a dick! Did he want me dead?

Jared's body went airborne, the scream wrenching my insides. He hit the wall with head and right shoulder, the scream cutting off.

"Jared!" I surged forward, only to realize this cage held an intense electric shock that knocked me on my ass.

Stunned, I followed Stefan with my eyes, his sword slicing through the air, his arms glowing in moving designs.

"Alas, we meet again," the hazel eyed man drawled, drawing a sword. His voice was like honey, but his movements resembled a badger. "How did you know I'd be here?"

"You reek of human death. You've gone too far, Andris, and for what results? I'm still better."

The two circled each other, their swords held loose. Both their steps were nimble and elegant, the more deadly for it.

"Tell me," the man said conversationally, "why waste power on that human female? Or did I go after the wrong human?"

"You? Make a mistake?"

"It is rare, yes, but when concerning humans, I'm sure you'll—"

Pale gold blade of the smooth talking man whipped out, aimed for Stefan's head. Stefan dodged, graceful like a dancer, joints moving as if oiled, then countering immediately.

The man dodged also, stepping away, forcing space between them. Assessing.

"Why wait, Andris?" Stefan asked, eyes calculating. "Why stall? What are you after?"

"Unsolved mysteries. For example, that male seemed rather usual, as far as humans go. Crying and begging—so much drama. Conversely, that female never showed fear. Then here you are, wasting valuable power to protect her. Is she a pet? Is that the draw? She certainly is pretty—I can see the allure. Maybe she wasn't scared because she thinks she is always protected?"

Stefan lunged, his sword swiped through the air. Andris dodged, the blade cutting through the air right next to his head. He countered immediately. Stefan met the attack and countered again, fast as lightning. Each time the blades met, sparks flew. The men evenly matched for height and brawn, but Stefan was faster and more skilled. Andris retreated, a step at a time, eyes darting, looking for a way out.

"Another time, then." Andris gave a slick smile.

I screamed as two more beings lumbered into the room, not much more than smoky wisps of purple. Both apparitions stopped at me, my chest once again surging outward, sensing something in them and wanting to call to it. Or maybe they called to me.

Before I could think more on it, one palpitating blob floated toward me like a plumb of smoke. I shrank back from the swirling burnished gold cage. Tendrils reached for me, connecting with magic. A spark lit up the room, the vapor creature flashing color and imploding, winking out.

Stefan flagged, momentarily slowed. Andris's blade found his flesh, slicing a huge red gash in his arm.

"No!" I screamed.

"And why do the *Dulcha* keep reacting to her?" Andris's voice became suspicious. "What have you found, Stefan? What is worth your life?"

Stefan switched his sword to his other arm, the color of the blade fading to orange. The cage around me did, too. His power was weakening as he tried to keep me out of harm's way.

Rage and fear consumed me in equal parts seeing Stefan struggling. I registered the look of triumph on Andris's face as he raised his sword. Without thinking I struck out, focused on that blade.

Black bands rose in the air around Andris like ribbons, wrapping around his sword and squeezing, breaking the blade into shards. Andris screamed and convulsed, drawing his sword arm into his chest, staring, wide-eyed, at his hand where my magic had burned him. His fingers shook, starting to turn a molten red. The color climbed, as if soaking into his skin, burning and blistering as it went.

Andris screamed, still staring, fixated.

Stefan, sword hanging loosely at his side, his face a blank mask. He was damn good at hiding his emotions.

I would have kept staring as well—I had no idea what I'd done—but the last blob of magic drifted toward me. I screamed again, drawing Stefan's gaze, scared that if it touched the cage something more would happen to him.

Charles burst through the door, blade whirling, cutting across the pouf of magic in his rage. His eyes swept the room, landing on a fleeing Andris. His gaze darted to Stefan, now hot on Andris's trail, then to me.

I spared a glance for Jared, his arms flailing limply. Good, he was alive.

I didn't get long for relief. Charles stared at me with crazy eyes.

I probably shouldn't have ditched him. He seemed slightly…perturbed.

"What the fuck, Sasha?"

Maybe more than slightly…

"You trying to get me fired?"

In three quick steps, he reached toward my neck, probably meaning something awful, only to hit Stefan's cage. A bright orange spark flared, singeing Charles's skin.

"Damn it! You come outta there because I got a score to settle with you! I want to shake you like a crying baby!"

"What a horrible thing to say!"

"Yeah! I am a freaking Watch Captain, Sasha! Yet I had to run down the street, in bare feet, naked, with nothing but a cell phone and a sword! Obviously I drew some notice! Plus, I had to go back to your damn apartment for a sword before I even followed you! It was locked!"

"You remembered your phone but not a sword? How is that my fault?"

"*Because you flustered me.* I'm going to—" Another flash of orange. "Damn it! You aren't worth his protection!"

"Another horrible thing. To think, I thought you liked me."

"You—"

Moaning interrupted my cringing from Charles. One of Jared's limbs tweaked. He moaned again.

"Go make sure he's okay," I instructed.

"No. And you know what, I don't even want to have sex with you anymore. That's how mad I am at you right now!"

"Over-dramatic, hmm?"

Stefan stepped into the room. He'd gone out through the window after Andris, he'd re-entered through the door. Judging by the lack of enemy blood, he didn't catch his prey. Judging by the huge gash on his arm that he tried to ignore, but brought protectively into his body, it hurt a lot.

His eyes found me, deep and dark.

"Can I get out, now?" I asked, shrinking back from his intense stare.

"Charles, grab Jared and get out."

Charles gave me a smug look of retribution before he did as instructed, gently lifting a moaning Jared and stalking from the apartment.

Stefan closed the door slowly, turning toward me and lowering to the ground, legs crossed. He stared at me through his self-made jail cell. "You…used magic. You attacked with magic."

"I didn't mean to! Well, yes I did. I just wanted him to stop hurting you. He was about to kill you!"

Stefan's eyes squinted. He leaned forward. "Are you okay?"

"Scared, a little. But…" Sweat dripped down my temple but I started to shiver. I looked at my arms. They glistened with moisture. My cheeks burned right before my head swirled.

The fever gripped me.

Suddenly the cage disappeared and Stefan had me in his arms. The last thing I remembered, he was running.

*****

"She's lucid, sir. Somewhat. No response, though."

Stefan approached the wide bed, looking down on the limp human, her angelic face devoid of color. Her arms rested on her chest, her body so still she looked dead.

A shot of fear pierced Stefan's chest. "Will she make it?"

Luke's head shook before he sighed. "She shouldn't have made it last time. Yet she did. Something is holding her to this life."

"My blood helped last time. Will it help again?"

Luke studied him, trying to read Stefan. He'd keep on trying, too. Stefan didn't maintain a leadership role by giving away his motives.

Stefan hadn't told anyone what he'd seen: That Sasha had used the black magic level, the most powerful, rarest level of magic that existed. That level of magic, nearly a pure shot drawn directly from the elements, hadn't been seen in hundreds of years—the use of it not more than legend. Even Trek, the enemy's mage, could only go as high as white, a step down.

"If you give her too much, too often, you will develop a link to her," Luke cautioned.

Stefan remained immobile. They already had a link. Before they'd even met they had a link. Another thing he didn't feel the need to divulge. "I understand."

Luke's head tilted. "This is extreme for a pet, don't you think? She's pretty," he shrugged, "but she is still just a human. They die early, they can rarely access their magic with any consistency… Plus, this human has caused a rare amount of trouble. I would advise you to reconsider."

Stefan barely kept his eyes from drifting to Sasha's face. "How many pets have I had, Luke?"

The doctor's eyes squinted marginally, thinking. His eyebrows rumpled.

"Exactly none. I don't keep pets. They are a nuisance and a waste of time, not to mention dangerous if they fall in love. As I'm sure you agree, humans can be unpredictable when they love or hate. Especially both at the same time. She is not a pet. I have had no interaction with her sexually. This is business, and she needs to live. Will my blood work?"

Luke sighed, raising his eyebrows in a facial shrug. "*If* you can get her to drink, she might pull out of it. *Might*. She should be dead already. But…well, she survived last time, so who's to say?"

While some cultures of human did ingest blood regularly, it was the blood of cattle or goat, and generally localized to that culture. Most of the time, a person or animal had to have specialized digestive mechanisms to filter out the excess iron consumed in blood. If they didn't, a person could easily sustain an iron overdose. Just another difference between humans and his species.

Luckily, Sasha's body had proved to be able to handle his blood, which was both high in power and highly taboo to most human cultures. He didn't understand why, but given the circumstances, it would save her life. Again. Hopefully.

Stefan nodded, allowing himself to bestow his gaze back to this woman that had a firm hold on his vitals for reasons he couldn't understand or explain. The only thing he knew with certainty was that she could not die. Not just for her magic ability, but also because…

Stefan shook his head. He refused to think about it. This was business, she was a rare find, that the enemy now had wind of, and she could-not-die!

"Get out," Stefan barked. He swung his gaze around the room to the half-dozen attendees.

As expected, everyone scattered, including the meddling Luke.

Stefan approached the bed slowly, his body tingling, his dick starting to pound. He should feed her his wrist. That's what he'd done before. There was distance in the wrist—an arm's length to be precise.

But he wanted to be closer. He wanted to be *inside* her while she drank his life's blood. Unfortunately, that would be similar to tricking her, since his pheromones didn't work on her and she would never consent to it with her boyfriend still in the picture. Damn unfortunate, because he knew she wanted him. Her self-control was just as slippery around him as his was around her.

He stripped his shirt and pants and crawled under the sheets, stretching out his bare body next to hers. He would bring her to his neck, only touching G-rated parts even though her clothes had been removed, and if she reacted so be it.

He slid his hand along her flat stomach, spreading out his fingers so he covered as much skin as possible. The length of his body touched hers, her skin soft and supple. She let out a faint, melodious moan. She turned on her side, breasts flattening against his chest. The need to crawl on top of her and plunge into her feminine depths nearly overcame him. He squeezed his eyes shut, holding back with everything he had.

He jabbed the right spot on his throat with his dagger before throwing it across the floor and out of the way. Bending quickly before control completely fled, he gently pulled her upper body up his chest so his neck butted against her lips.

Her hands came up weakly, trying to bat him away, her lips curling under to shut her mouth tight.

"C'mon, Sasha, just a little bit." Stefan held her tight against him, her lips pressed against his neck where a slow trickle of liquid begged her to suck.

She opened her mouth, but with the intention to kiss him rather than drink. Her smooth lips grazed his skin, firing up his body and making his erection throb uncomfortably. Her mouth fastened over the cut, her tongue flicking at the liquid. With a soft moan, her lips applied pressure. Glorious suction pulled at his body, reaching all the way down to the center of his being and tugging. His cock jerked, the tip tingling.

She sucked harder, rendering a moan from him this time, his hands sliding over her well-proportioned hip and down to her butt. Having lost control of his limbs in the sheer pleasure of the draw from her lips, he pulled her lower half closer, his cock sliding into the space between her upper thighs.

"Mmm," she breathed, back to kissing him instead of drinking.

"Drink more, love. You need more of me to heal."

Her hand felt up his chest, her delicate fingers tracing his muscles, stopping on his flexing pec. Eyes closed, she bent her head to him again, the fire from her mouth consuming him. His fingers worked in between her butt cheeks, circling that small hole lightly. His cock skimmed her wet sex, working against it, parting her outer lips.

She groaned, taking a long, deep pull from his neck. She let go of his neck with a pop, her tongue flowing over her bottom lip, clearing it of the last drops of him. Against his neck she murmured, "Take me."

He lost his shit.

Feeling like she yanked a string directly tied to his stomach and cock, he rolled on top of her, flame licking his skin where she touched. Her hands glided up his arms, over his shoulders, over his neck, and to his head. She pulled him toward her.

Stefan allowed her to lead, sinking between her spread legs, his manhood pressed heavily against her heat soaked, wet sex. He couldn't remember ever being this wild; this desperate to take a female. He pounded with it. Throbbed.

Her lips touched his lightly, assessing. Her tongue darting out to lick his lips, tasting. More pressure, their mouths opening to each other. Her tongue entered his mouth, seeking him, and then drawing him out. Playful and fun, experimenting. She tasted like chocolate, spice, and his essence, she smelled like fresh everglades in the crisp dusk.

His hips pushed forward, his tip parting her folds, her heat scorching him pleasantly. Further still, her body so tight he wasn't able to push any farther without causing her pain.

Her head fell back. A small smile played around her lips as her chest heaved and her legs climbed up his hips. She was trying to work him in. In the meantime, she was driving him fucking wild!

Sweat beaded his brow, dripping down with the exertion of pulling out that two inches, then slowly, grindingly, threading it back in, allowing her to wiggle and squirm, trying to get it deeper.

"Ohhhh!" Her breath wound around his head dizzyingly, flirting with his ears. Her smell, so intense, he wanted to stop breathing lest he thrust into her blindly, stealing his willpower.

"*More*," she whispered.

He pushed in slowly, his body quivering, needing release with a fervor that wasn't natural. He was halfway there, stretching her, filling her, getting squeezed by her. Fuck he was getting squeezed! How could a person be so *tight* and not be a virgin? Madness.

Speaking of madness, his sanity slipped. He pulled out, his body slick with sweat, his hands braced on each side of her. Taking her tightening of arms and legs as they wrapped around him, he pushed in again, riding low, laying his body on hers but keeping his weight off by his taxed arms.

"All the way." Her voice drifted over him like smoke, infused by her smell, and flicked away the last trace of constraint.

He thrust in desperation, emotion riding the action. His cock burrowed into her tight depths, making her squeal as he forced her to accept him. He paused a second, his dick wrapped in an earth-shattering, liquid fire, before pulling out again, starting a slow rhythm.

Her hands clutched at him, her mouth seeking his. He met her lips, their tongues dancing, their bodies grinding together pleasantly; a thick fog of pleasure covering his awareness. He thrust blindly, over and over, the friction of her, the intoxication, driving all thought from his mind.

"Oh, yes," Sasha said into his mouth, her eyes fluttered. "Oh…"

Stefan deepened the kiss, wanting to take her blood as well. He wanted to exchange their power, merge it, become one with it.

Before he'd realized what had happened, his mouth was at her throat, her hands at the back of his head, pulling down, wanting this as much as he did. He barely registered the blaring siren in the back of his head. If he took what little strength she had, he'd kill her.

Ripping his head away, shivers covering his body, then heat, he regained his control. She clutched at him, dragging his body closer, wanting as much contact as possible. His body pushed down deep, trying to hit the center of her. Her hips swiveled up to meet his, accepting his manhood in surges. He plunged and retreated, filling every inch of her. Raw desire fueled her frantic movements, having her panting and sweaty, moaning. Her eyebrows lifted, her expression turned to anticipated wonder. Her legs tightened, her fingernails dug into him.

"Going to…*oh!*" Her body shuddered, her already tight core constricting like a fist.

His body blasted apart, his cock shooting his seed deep into her, pumping it deeper still, needing a piece of him to remain within her as long as possible. Knowing that that wasn't enough. Knowing he'd only be content if he remained in her forever.

He let his body push her down into the mattress, trapping her under him, unlocking a secretion that his race hardly ever used. He remained within her, meeting her lips and holding, while the primal side of him slipped out from under his logic. She was his. He'd always known it. So had she. It was as permanent in their hearts as it was now in their bodies. Fate had chosen.

So he let the primal side take over, lowering his neck to her once again, needing her to take more.

Chapter Seventeen

I awoke with a glorious stretch. "Ow."

"Serves you right." Charles sat in a chair off to the side, his knitting needles clicking.

"I'm sore." Which was an understatement. Every single muscle felt like it'd been stretched.

Speaking of stretched... My lady bits ached, as if I'd been violated in the most pleasant of ways.

A dream came back to me, of Stefan moving over me, crushing me to the mattress, my body entwined with his. It had been the best dream I had ever had, equipped with the absolutely best orgasm I could imagine.

"Did..." This was going to sound really dumb. "Did the Boss...hang out in here? At all?"

Charles didn't even look up. "Yup. He gave you more blood, pissing off that super bitch Darla to no end, and saved your life, yet again. Not that you deserved it."

"How long are you going to be mad at me, exactly?"

"At least another day, then I'll see how I feel."

"You didn't have sex with me, did you?"

I got a scathing glance. "As it stands, I will only consent to screw you because it would be a waste to refuse, but I will still be pissed."

So no, then. "Huh."

Click, click, click.

He tilted his head marginally, as if he couldn't help asking, "So, does that mean you're offering?"

I scoffed at him as I sat up slowly, my body feeling strung out and my lady bits sending shooting remembrances of pleasure to my body. "The Boss didn't…"

The glance was sardonic this time. "He barely screws people of his own caliber, let alone dumb humans that ditch their faithful, *loyal* guards for a ridiculous human boyfriend that always manages to need a woman's help. Talk about thinking highly of yourself…"

Right. That's what I'd figured; but still, I was sore. Maybe it was just an effect of the magic. The rest of my body felt beat to hell, why not that part as well?

I tossed it out of my mind, stowing that delicious dream to the back of my head for later remembrance when I had some alone time to take matters into my own hands. My mind drifted to Jared. I cringed.

"How's Jared?" I asked in a tiny voice.

Click, click, click.

"I'll blow you for information…" I kept my voice even. He was just young enough to believe me.

"Lies."

Or not.

"Jared has made a full recovery. This time. What's going to happen next time…? I wonder. It isn't him they're after. For some stupid reason…"

I sighed. He'd hit directly on the problem. Since my infatuation with Stefan, and more so when I went searching for the living shadows, he'd been in danger constantly. I'd had to try and save him just as often. For a girl who could barely walk in a straight line without getting sidetracked by moving objects in the darkness, I wasn't the best person to hang his hope on. Oh yeah, and I had no fighting skills, no arsenal besides a whistle and a letter opener, and no muscles. Jared was in the wrong hands.

I loved him, but I couldn't play this game with him anymore. I didn't know what my life held in store for me, but I had a feeling that, with that knitting oaf following me around, and my wires constantly crossing with a guy that tugged at the fibers of my being every time I saw him, it wouldn't be normal.

All Jared had ever wanted was a wife, house, picket fence, and family. And while I might want that, too, I would have to go about it in a very different way. Part of me always suspected that— the part that figured I'd never have those things.

"Why were they after you, anyway?" Charles had lowered his pastime to stare at me.

I sighed, trying not to let my sinking heart squeeze out tears. Charles wouldn't understand. "Because I rock, that's why. Can you show me to Jared's room?"

"Whatever gets you to stop the terrible jokes?"

Ten minutes later I sat in front of Jared at a tiny table used for teatime. As such, delicate cups with pastel flowers adorned polished, mahogany wood. Books sprawled behind us, lining giant, floor to ceiling bookcases.

Jared's eyes stared at me with equal parts wariness and distance. A chunk of his hair was missing, leaving an angry red patch of scalp in its place. A bandaged wrapped around his shoulder, a Band-Aid by his ear. I hadn't even opened my mouth and my heart ached.

"Hi, how are you feeling?" I started in a gentle voice.

"Does *he* have to be here?" Jared hid a point under the table, his finger aimed at Charles in the corner, back to his knitting.

I nodded sadly. "He's here to protect us."

Jared shook his head sadly. "I can't handle any more of this, Sasha. I wake up forgetting, then I end up in horrible situations where everything comes tumbling back. Then I forget again. I can't do it anymore."

"I know, baby. It's my fault. All of this. It's all my fault."

"I always thought you were eccentric, with your imaginary men in the shadows. I thought you lived in a secret romance novel or something. But this…I just…I can't keep up, you know? We aren't the same people anymore. At least…well…*I* am, I think, but…"

He let the words trail into the air, hanging, sprinkling guilt down onto me like the first rain drops before a storm.

I hung my head.

"I've been offered a great opportunity in Florida," he went on, "and I think I'm going to take it."

My head snapped up. "A job?"

"Yes, a job. I think I should take it."

"But…how? When?"

Jared reached forward to pat my arm, but stopped halfway and lowered his hand into his lap. "It's for the best. I hold you back…maybe. I think. Just…this is for the best."

I stared at him in something close to disbelief. A heavy weight filled my chest. We'd been together for years. He'd been my *first*. I'd learned to partially trust with him. I learned what love was supposed to be. Sadly, I also learned that love was beyond my ability to grasp.

He was right. He needed a stable woman with no demons. With no weird past and strange magical abilities. Even if I hadn't stumbled into this world where I now found myself, we wouldn't have worked out. We were different in our very foundations, in different worlds.

This really sucked.

As a tear leaked down my face, I said, "I didn't know about any of this, Jared, if that's what you think."

"I think I know that, Sasha. I just… You're too…sparkly. You just…we don't fit anymore. You grew into your body, and I…well, I'm still just the same ol' me."

I wanted to argue with this absurdity. With this nonsense. But I also knew that my future would only drag him down; drag him into danger. It was time for us to part ways. I needed to let him go, and it would be easiest on him if he had no resistance. If I didn't cause him to doubt. I knew this, but…

But *God* it hurt.

I sucked in a big, sob ridden breath. "I don't know what to say."

He smiled, his eyes glassy. "How about goodbye?"

The second tear fell, followed by many others. I bowed my head, moving to him painfully. My arms wrapped around his neck, our cheeks touching. After a minute, he disentangled me, and I moved away, my eyes overflowing.

Jared got up slowly, painfully. With a final smile—the smile I had grown to depend on these last few years—he walked out of the room. The heavy door closed with a faint click.

I bowed my head into my hands, letting go. He'd been *my everything*. I had lain in his bed, looking out the window, talking about my dreams, and then listening to his. I had learned to trust, to depend on someone. He had been a huge chunk of my life.

I heard movement before two strong arms came around me. Charles held me tight, patting my back awkwardly like the young guy he was. I sobbed into his chest, my heart aching as part of myself walked away forever.

*****

Stefan's eyes snapped open as dusk fell. He had a ton to do tonight. His enemy continued to roam his territory and prey on his people without his people sensing the territory breach. He needed to stop that; give his clan back their reassurance.

He also needed to figure out the new situation with the human.

Snapping straight, sheets falling away, he thought back to the night before. He'd pushed himself on a weak, vulnerable woman. He had acted like a drunk teenager rather than the leader of this territory!

And he'd marked her.

Stefan groaned. What had he been thinking?

But that was just it—with her, he found thinking difficult. But marking just wasn't done anymore. Their clan—their race, actually--was sexually liberated. Multiple partners at any given time, his clan held nothing back, experimenting and engaging as often, with however many, as possible. A long time ago, when the humans ravaged their numbers in crusades and witch burnings, their current sexual outlook had saved their race from extinction; sex as often as possible, without pregnancy-hindering protection, meant his race started to bounce back.

Now it was a *thing.* It felt good, it helped identify possible breeders, and it was to everybody's gain.

He'd nearly ended that for Sasha. Granted, she wasn't of his race, but she exhibited traits his clan could understand and appreciate. Even though she didn't understand her sexual side, like her fearlessness, it lurked. It popped its head up and played peek-a-boo every time sex tumbled into the room.

Or even just when Stefan hesitantly wandered close to her.

Damn it! Just thinking of her gave him wood.

Her only saving grace: he didn't take her blood. He didn't complete the marking. Not yet. At this half-done job, his clan would sense his presence around her, like a ghost sitting on her shoulder, but it wouldn't be an open challenge if they touched her.

Stefan clenched his jaw and breathed through his nose. She was *his*. Something deep and primal knew that. Had faith in it. He wasn't sure what he would do if she chose another.

Yes he did—he would challenge that male and rip his throat out.

Stefan took another deep breath. His life had been hard enough without her barging in and confusing it all to hell. And now she had some pretty potent magic. Worse, Andris suspected it. What a pain.

Showered and dressed, Stefan waltzed out of his room. He crossed the campus of their estate, ducked into a hidden door, and walked into Sasha's room a moment later, ignoring Charles as he bounded up.

Sasha sat in a large velvet chair across the room, her eyes bloodshot and puffy, a book open on her lap. A cotton pajama set covered her body from head to toe, only her hands, feet and face peeking out. Her hair hid within a towel.

She looked up, sadness radiating through their new blood line, intensified by their normal link.

"Sasha." His voice carried across the room. Testing the waters.

A spark ignited in her gaze, then dulled immediately. "Hey. Sorry I nearly got you killed."

"I trust you...slept well?" Stefan asked evenly. *Do you know that we slept together? That I want to do it again?*

She shrugged, her gaze sinking to her book. "Thanks for saving my life. Again."

He crossed the room, taking a chair next to hers. "You're sad. Why?"

She shrugged again. "I ended it with Jared. Well, not true. He ended it with me. So, I guess it was mutual, all said and done."

Sorrow radiated, this time accompanied by her bottom lip quivering. Stefan had an impulse to wrap her in his arms until she cried herself healthy.

Deep breath.

"Why did you end it?"

He listened as Sasha recounted the story. Nowhere in there that she'd cheated. Not even a hint. Finally, he tiptoed closer to the mark. "How is your body today? Are you sore?"

Her eyes showed the first glimmer of suspicion. "Why?"

"Last time this happened you could barely move. I'm wondering if you're adjusting."

Suspicion winked out. "Oh. I'm okay. Much the same."

She didn't know. How could she not know? She'd never opened her eyes, but she'd spoken to him. She'd directed him!

His heart sank before he could get himself back online. How had this female—this *human* female—worked so thoroughly past his defenses and captured him? It was stupid and dangerous, both for his rank and his way of life. It needed to end. *Now.*

*****

I watched in confusion as Stefan's face and body language shut down. He looked pissed. At me?

"You okay?" I ventured.

"Great." His jaw tightened as his shoulders hunched. "Look, I'll cut to the chase. You're in danger. The enemy, E.T., now have an interest in you. You demonstrated magic in front of them. They'll return for you—"

"Wait." I held up my hand in disbelief. "Did you just say *ET*?"

Stefan's eyebrows made a flat line over his eyes. "Yes…"

"As in *ET phone home…?*" I felt like crap, my heart hurt, Stefan had a stronger tug than normal, nearly rising me out of my chair to connect my body with his, but suddenly none of that mattered in the spotlight of this absurdity.

Or maybe I needed something to focus on that *didn't* matter.

Stefan shook his head, his gaze flicking to Charles. Knitting needles stilled as Charles tilted his head.

"Don't you guys ever watch movies?" I asked.

Their eyebrows looked like sheets billowing in the wind. They had no idea what I was talking about.

"Right. Anyway. Continue." I waved Stefan on diplomatically. Charles rolled his eyes.

"Anyway, the Eastern Territory has an interest. They won't stop trying to acquire you until that interest is extinguished, whether by them kidnapping you, killing you, or killing us all."

"Lovely. You should know, they've been trying to take me with them since that first monster-thing talked to me."

Charles dropped his knitting in surprise, but Stefan just nodded. "What did it say?"

"Well, basically that I should join it— them—for vast rewards and what not."

Stefan nodded uncomfortably as Charles gawked.

"So...I'm a freak, then?" I looked back and forth between the two, my heart sinking. "I'm still a freak, even with you guys?"

It was Stefan that recovered first. "No. Extremely valuable, though I don't have the expertise to know what exactly that means." His leadership mask clicked on. "No matter. You will need protection. You will live here, in this room, using this area for your—"

"No." I crossed my arms.

Stefan's stare hardened. "I don't hear the term 'no' often…"

"It isn't a term, it's a word. And…no."

Charles started to fidget.

Stefan flexed from head to toe. Each powerful muscle on his giant frame snapped to attention. I gasped, my sexy systems swelling, the ache in those sexy systems more pronounced. I suddenly needed him inside me with a ferocity that both terrified and excited me. My cheeks flushed and my head beaded in sweat. My body and soul both seemed to be screaming *destiny!* The pain from losing Jared was still so acute, but when presented with Stefan…I couldn't explain it. My being didn't want anyone else. I only wanted him.

Charles groaned in the corner.

"You will live here. End of story." Stefan's jaw clenched again, as did his fists. The pupils in those dark eyes, barely definable, got larger.

I wanted to get up and walk to him. Drape myself across him. Feel his arms tighten around me and make everything okay. *Destiny!*

"Boss, I might need to step outside…" Charles groaned through tight vocal chords.

Stefan looked like he was wrestling with something. Probably the memory of that stupid, although gorgeous, woman that had a claim on him. He shook his head in two jerks. "We're almost done."

His eyes honed in on me. "You leave here, you die. Even if you manage to fight back with magic, the fever that follows will kill you if someone powerful isn't around to…help you…" Lust flashed before a scowl reformed. "You will die. Which means you stay. You stay, you learn to use your power, and you advance. If you can reach the end of the lessons without killing yourself, you are free to go. That good?"

"Well…let me think…." I was poking the bear in the nose with a stick, yes, but defiance was my go-to defense mechanism. Besides, I didn't feel in control of my life anymore. It was worrying. "I've survived this long. I'll take my chances a little longer. So, thank you, but still no."

"Or, you will go home, find a few *monsters,* as you call them, and get captured. Trek has no shortage of creations to send your way."

"I'll keep her here, Boss," Charles said with bravado.

He *so* wouldn't.

Stefan's eyes still delved into mine as he said, "You will be attending school with her. You will eat and breathe each other—"

He cut off. His eyes closed, as if pain lanced his body. He sucked in a deep breath. A moment later he relaxed. "You two will go to school together, live here together, and come out better for it."

"But, I've already been to school," Charles whined.

"You have learning to do, and I have a feeling Sasha will push you to greater heights."

By the shake in Charles' head, he didn't have the same ideas.

Stefan got up to leave. I wanted to stop him. I wanted to talk to him about these feelings—even though it was a little awkward with Charles in the room. Before he left, though, he said, "Oh, and Sasha, your apartment had a forced entry. A fire started shortly thereafter. Jared is leaving, so you say. Where will you go, if not here?"

All the thoughts fell out of my head. The click of the latch as he left was surprisingly loud.

My gaze slowly traveled the walls, taking my time in disbelief, landing on a cringing Charles. "You forced entry. What is this about a fire?"

Charles tried to sink into himself, an impossible feat for a muscular man over six-and-a-half feet tall. "I *may* have, accidentally, left a candle burning."

"When we left there were no candles lit…"

"I *may* have lit one so I could see."

"I have electricity, Charles. Why would you need to light a candle?"

"Lights are so bright!"

I started to hyperventilate. Everything I owned was in that apartment. All my memories, all my knick-knacks, all the things I had collected throughout my life, sat on my shelves or in my cubbies. I didn't have a whole lot, but now I had nothing.

"How much of the apartment burned?" I asked quietly.

Charles slouched lower. "About three-fourths."

Three-fourths of my whole life, gone. Just like that.

It wasn't the happy-go-lucky Destiny at all, at least not in this. Destiny's cousin, the mean and often brutal, Fate had left me no way out.

All my life I'd seen the shadow men roaming the darkness. I'd seen human shaped silhouettes where everyone else had seen nothing at all. I'd always wondered, about them and about my sanity. And when it came right down to it, I knew I belonged here like I'd never belonged anywhere else before. I knew that my secret box would be largely understood within this new fold of people. I wouldn't have to hide, anymore. I wouldn't have to worry about people locking me up.

I sighed and looked around at my new life. Clean surfaces and empty shelves stared back. It was bare bones, like I was brand new. Basically, I was starting from scratch.

But at least I had something to work from. Stefan saw something in me. He would've given his life to protect me. That had to be something. His faith didn't seem easily bestowed. If I truly did have magic, then I could truly fit in. Right now I was a freak human, sure; but if I could prove myself an asset, I could be a cool foreigner. Maybe I could finally be good at something. I could finally let myself trust and form real friendships, or meet a guy I didn't have to hide half myself from.

My mind flashed to Stefan—to the dream of him. I felt him moving away from me, leaving the area and going about his business. I still had no idea how.

Glass barely half full, I lay down, my head starting to pound.

"Can you make me forget?" I asked Charles quietly.

"That doesn't work on you."

"It works long enough to help me go to sleep."

"I'll try. Usually you have to be strung out and not anticipating me. But I'll try."

I closed my eyes and let blackness consume me, closing the chapter on my old life. I'd found my shadow men, and they'd opened a new chapter in my life.

THE END

Sasha's journey continues in:

Braving the Elements

Sasha has always known she was different, but now she also knows that the shadow men she's seen all her life, are real.

With a life goal of fitting in, Sasha hopes her strange abilities will finally make true friendship a possibility. Unfortunately, her magic doesn't function like everyone else's. What she thought would make her belong, sets her apart now more than ever.

Stefan, all but promised to a different woman, has tried to keep his mind on his duties instead of the irresistible and free-spirited human. But when she is threatened, he can't keep his distance anymore. He'll stop at nothing to keep her safe, and more importantly, make her his.

Just when one thing clicks into place, another spirals out of control. Stefan's clan isn't the only group that would benefit from an extremely rare type of magic. And their enemies will stop at nothing to get what they want

Excerpt:

A boy in front of us pushed his friend. "You were the *last one.* What an idiot!"

"Shut up," the other boy spat. "I wasn't raised with an older brother like you were—how could I've known how? And besides, the human didn't get it at all."

"The human doesn't count. And hardly anyone has an older brother. Idiot!"

"Shut the hell up or I'm going to shove my foot up your ass!"

The first boy laughed harder, taunting. They would've gotten in a fight right there if not for Charles grabbing each by their shirts and tossing one first, and then the other, out the door. Limbs went flying.

"Don't worry about them, Sasha," Charles said in a low tone for my ears alone. "We know you can do it. You're just new to all this. You'll figure it out."

I shrugged.

"Stop shrugging and have some faith in yourself."

Jared said that to me all the time. Have faith in myself. I'd always commented that it was his job. And he always had. Except now, he was gone.

We hit the first floor. I paused, feeling that familiar tug from the back of the house. Where we should be headed for dinner, or to just go to bed. A glance told me the weird connection to Stefan was right—he stood in the center of the wide hallway, his body pointed directly at me, his eyes boring into mine. Like Moses parting the seas, people gave him a wide berth, his advisors standing by like a swat team on steroids.

He probably wanted to check up on his investment; find out what saving my life had yielded.

Goose egg, that's what.

Pity party. Who brought the confetti?

"Can you beguile cops into deciding they shouldn't hand out tickets for going outrageously fast?" I asked Charles, not really caring if he could or not.

"Uh…maybe we should head toward the Boss. He seems… I think he wants you to go that way. See how your first class went…"

"My, my, Charles. I had no idea your analytical skills could deduce the obvious. Well done."

"I don't like this defiance thing you got going with him. Someone's going to get hurt, and it's probably going to be me."

"I thought you wanted a little excitement."

"Excitement, Sasha. I didn't say public execution."

Stefan kept staring, the pull on my chest trying to drag my body toward him. And there was absolutely nothing in the entire world I wanted more than to let him fold me in his arms and make everything all right; to smooth all this away. But I would just be the human who got special treatment from the Boss—assuming he'd even leave his drop-dead gorgeous girlfriend and play nursemaid to a pain in the ass. His help would look like a hand-out if he stooped low enough to give it.

Jesus. Forget a pity party, I was throwing myself a pity bonanza.

"I'm going to get in my car and drive really, really fast. As in danger-ville fast. Can you keep the cops from hauling me to jail?"

"Yeah," he whined, staring at Stefan.

"Then let's go for a ride. Speed always makes me feel better."

<u>Braving the Elements</u>

~~~~~~

Contacting K.F. Breene:
Website: kfbreene.com
Blog: kfbreene.org
Facebook: www.facebook.com/authorKF
Twitter: @KFBreene

To be put on the mailing list (for new releases and giveaways):
http://www.kfbreene.com/mailing-list.html

Printed in Great Britain
by Amazon.co.uk, Ltd.,
Marston Gate.